# A BOWL OF Friends

## "Friends are Forever"

LINDA,

THANKS for Being A friend.

Terry

Written By Terry Delaney
Illustrations By Nadia Ronquillo
Character Development, Erik Rosenblum

A Bowl of Friends: "Friends are Forever"
© 2021 Terry Delaney

First Edit 10 May, 2021

Written By Terry Delaney
Illustrations By Nadia Ronquillo
Character Development, Erik Rosenblum

Library of Congress Control Number: 2023910363

ISBN: 979-8-218-21082-3

# CHAPTER 1

Betty the Bowl was born in a dark, spooky, tin-and-brick factory that sat alone on a deserted street. The factory looked old enough to have been built when the horse and buggy ruled the roads. No one knows how or why the factory survived the wrecking ball that demolished all the buildings around it.

A tall chain-link fence topped with barbwire, deadly as sharks' teeth, surrounded the factory. A large "Beware of Dog" sign hung near the entrance, daring anyone to venture onto the lot. A plume of black smoke constantly billowed from the tall brick chimney, visible from miles away. The nasty smoke sometimes hung over the nearby town like a dark cloud, putting everyone in a gloomy mood. No one ever had a nice thing to say about that old, decrepit factory.

A story is told that one evening, four kids, one of them a girl named Betty, dared one another to sneak through a broken part of the fence. The children were never seen again, and it's said that their parents could sometimes see their children's faces reflected in the shiny silver bowls made in that factory.

Inside the building was a maze of large belts, grinders, and stampers, along with fire and smoke. None of the big burly workers, dressed in hard hats, goggles, and heavy gloves, ever looked up or smiled. They could've been zombies!

At one end of the factory, a big mess of rusted scrap metal looked like a shipwreck lying in its ocean grave. Workers threw scraps from the pile into a gigantic crusher that chewed them into small pieces, like a dinosaur happily attacking its prey.

The scraps were then dumped into a fiery, bubbling vat, stirred like a bowl of pancake batter, pressed into flat sheets, and almost instantly recycled into new bright silver bowls.

One normal, gloomy work day, a factory inspector with heavy gloves and a grumpy face picked up a freshly-made bowl, whose name was Betty. He barely looked at her, ignoring her beautiful smile, and tossed her onto the fast-moving conveyor belt. Betty tried to say "thank you," but sadly the harried inspector wasn't interested in a talking bowl.

Betty was quickly thrust into a box, which was dropped onto a pallet, labeled, and stacked in the warehouse. Betty's box was on top of the stack, so she could move around a little. All Betty wanted was out ... now! The darkness was scary and she was alone. With all her might, Betty struggled to break through the box, but it was too strong. Her escape would have to wait – but how, and when?

An angry voice rang out through the loud clatter of the factory: "Get that truck loaded and out of here!"

Suddenly Betty could feel her world moving and thought, Where am I going? It was all so confusing. She was tossed and tumbled as her box was loaded onto a truck, which headed out through the gate at a crazy, unsafe speed.

*No need to stop at the guard gate*, Charlie the truck driver figured. The guard would be asleep, or texting his friends. As always, Charlie took the turn out of the factory way too fast, tipping onto two wheels and almost turning the truck over. He was lucky to have won another battle with gravity. *Wow, for a second, I was on two wheels. That was fun! Maybe if I go a little faster next time, I can drive on two wheels longer!* He never thought that next time, gravity might win and the truck would tip right over. Charlie was very foolish.

In the back of the truck, boxes tumbled and tossed this way and that. Betty's box split open, and she flew right out of it and landed in a corner. Dazed and dented, Betty frowned for the first time in her life.

*I like smiling much better*, Betty thought, unaware that the new small dent on her shiny surface would change the course of her life.

# CHAPTER 2

As he backed the truck up to the store's loading dock, Charlie suspected there could be a real mess in the back thanks to his reckless driving. It wasn't the first time he hit that corner like he was driving a racecar instead of a delivery truck. He could lose his job for that, but Charlie always had a sneaky backup plan. He would just open the back of the truck before the owner of the store came out, and rearrange the boxes as if nothing had happened.

As quickly as possible and with a big evil smile, Charlie began his backup plan. Sure that he'd get away with things once again, he opened the back of the truck, expecting it to look like a tsunami had hit. But he found only a few boxes scattered about.

One bowl was lying on the floor of the truck. That was Betty, and she had a dent on her lip. She was okay but a little mad! Betty knew exactly what Charlie was up to as he picked her up with his cold hands and stuffed her quickly back into her box.

"No one will ever know," he said, laughing to his oh-so-clever self. His plan would remove all evidence of his dangerous driving.

"You're late again," said the owner of the store, his stern tone startling Charlie.

"Oh, sorry, sir, but a car pulled out in front of me and I barely escaped hitting it!"

"Well, glad you're okay," the owner said.

"Oh yes, sir. I am, too." Charlie turned his back to the storeowner as he grabbed the box with Betty inside. He grinned again. If anyone noticed the dent in the bowl, he'd blame it on the factory workers.

Betty heard the back door of the truck slam shut, smelled nasty exhaust fumes, and heard the tires screech as Charlie raced off again. Betty felt bad for all the bowls still in the truck and stuck with wicked Charlie.

She couldn't help feeling relieved she was free. But back in the dark box, she had no idea what would happen to her next.

# CHAPTER 3

Betty had been trapped in her box way too long. It wasn't until the next morning that a bell above the store's door broke the lonesome silence.

Welcoming voices soon filled the store, and Betty sensed right away that these people were very different from the factory workers. They seemed happy to be starting another day, and she sensed these folks were close friends.

Light was sneaking through the top of her box and she could hear window shades opening, letting in the warm morning sunshine. She heard country music playing and smelled the aroma of fresh coffee. *Oh, this is much better than the scary noises and burning smells of the factory!*

Betty was excited when someone said, "We need to put those items delivered yesterday on the shelf." She couldn't wait to see her new home, and was happy that her time as a captive would soon end.

Finally the box was opened and light shone off Betty's surface. Soft hands lifted her up and spun her around. Then a voice said, "Oh my, this bowl has a dent. I'll put it back in the box and take it over to the thrift shop later."

Betty felt sad and dejected. It seemed like no one wanted her.

But then the store's owner said something that lifted Betty's spirits. "I really like supporting the thrift store because it helps so many people in our community."

Hearing that the thrift store helped people in need gave Betty new hope. *Now that's a place I can't wait to visit.* Betty wanted to love everyone – except maybe that driver Charlie. And something down deep told her that helping is part of loving.

Later that afternoon, Betty was taken to the thrift store, where she was placed on a rack marked "SALE" at the back of the store.

I'm here on the sale rack, Betty thought, so I'll make the best of it.

# CHAPTER 4

Day after day, customer after customer walked by the sale rack without looking at Betty. But she didn't give up hope.

One day a salt-and-pepper set joined Betty on the sale rack. The two shakers were shaped and painted like little Mexican Chihuahuas, and the magnets on their noses made them appear to be kissing. The boy shaker was salt – you could tell because he had two holes in his sombrero. The girl shaker was pepper; she had three holes behind her beautiful piñata hair comb. Sadly, one of her Chihuahua ears had broken off, which was why the pair was put on the sale rack.

The colorful shakers were soon joined by two beautiful wooden salad servers shaped like hands. The right hand was unfortunately missing a finger.

Betty was delighted to have some new friends, even if they all were stuck on the sale rack in the lonely and forgotten space at the back of the store.

*It doesn't matter what rack we live on, she thought. What matters is how we live on that rack and help each other.*

"Oh, dios mio,' Salt said gloomily. 'We're on the sale rack! No one will love us here!"

Betty tried to say hi to her new friends – because everyone is a friend until they aren't – but no one heard her thanks to tearful Salt.

"We'll never make it to a Thanksgiving dinner table now," Salt said sadly. "No one gets to the big table from the sale rack."

"I'll never be able to toss the salad with a finger missing," added the right salad hand, sounding as mournful as Salt but using sign language, which is a way to communicate using only your hands.

The left salad hand quickly signed back. "You still have four fingers and they all work perfectly. You will be just fine."

Betty tried again. "Hi. I'm Betty the bowl."

The girl Chihuahua said, "Oh! I've never met a talking bowl before. Nice to meet you. I'm Pepper. Salt and I have been nose-to-nose for as long as I can remember."

Then the salad servers moved a little closer.

"Hey!" said Pepper. "You're walking upright, like us."

The right hand signed, "Yes, with a little limp and the help of my paper clip. But that won't stop me from tossing a beautiful salad someday."

The left hand signed, "We are Left and Right. We're from Hawaii."

Betty liked her new friends immediately. "Don't let a missing finger or a broken ear hold you back. I have a dent that I won't let keep me down. Someday we'll all be together at a Thanksgiving table, and a great day that will be! I promise." *I kind of remember a Thanksgiving ...*

Salt interrupted to moan, "We're never getting off this

sale rack. It's the junk yard!"

"Now, now, Salt. Calm down," said Pepper. "We can work in the kitchen just fine. Someone will see us and take us all home soon."

Betty wanted them to find a new home together more than anything in the world. But days passed, and more people just walked right by the sale rack. Betty didn't give up hope. In her heart, she knew she and her new friends were just as valuable as any other kitchen utensils in the store.

# CHAPTER 5

Winter turned into spring, spring turned into summer, and Betty still knew that someday, she and her friends would all leave the sale rack. In the meantime, the only thing that ever happened to them was being dusted by one of the store clerks. Pepper called it a dust storm, but Betty knew it made them look a little nicer.

When you spend time together, you learn a lot about each other. Betty was the first to tell her friends about herself, describing the old, rundown factory where her story began. "You would not believe how terrifying that big metal crusher was," she said. "It shook the whole building with every bite, like a T Rex. And the flaming molten steel was as hot as the sun. The workers had to wear protective clothing, goggles and gas masks when they worked near it."

Pepper said, *"Dios mío, qué horror!"*

"And the most awful thing was being stuffed in a dark box not knowing where I was headed, and then being tossed around in the back of a delivery truck," Betty said. "I'm still mad at that crazy truck driver."

Salt couldn't hold back any longer. "I can't believe something so good and beautiful as you, Betty, was made in that awful old factory."

One night, Salt and Pepper told their story. It was as if they were singing a love song in two-part harmony. They were made, or as they put it, "born," in a little Mexican factory, and purchased by a nice family on vacation. "Oh, we were so lucky," they both said.

"We had the honor of joining the family at each meal, for many years," Pepper said.

"And then one day Pepper lost an ear unexpectedly," Salt continued. "We could not believe when we were tossed in the trash. No way were we going to the dump ..."

"So we had to move quickly," they said together.

"When the coast was clear, we climbed out of the trashcan under the kitchen sink ..." Salt explained.

"And we hid in a box labeled 'Thrift Store'," Pepper finished. "Little did we know we would end up on this sale rack."

In a reassuring voice, Betty said, "You guys will never have to worry about being dumped again. We're family now."

Later that night, Left and Right signed their story. It came as naturally to them as playing the ukulele. And Left and Right explained that, like some ukuleles, they were made of the special Koa wood, which in the Hawaiian culture represents integrity and strength. The word Koa also means brave, bold, and fearless.

"Our family could no longer afford to live in Hawaii, so one day our world was packed up in a steel container, placed on a big ship, and headed out to sea. During the long voyage to our new home, the sea turned into a dark

14

and wild monster and tossed the huge ship around as if it was a little rowboat. One day when the storm was at its peak, an iron teapot packed just above us fell on Right and broke off one of his fingers. When our family arrived at our new home, we were unpacked and our owners discovered Right was missing a finger, so they donated us to this thrift store."

"It could have been a lot worse, though. We might have been used for firewood!" Left said as Right nodded.

Betty, Salt and Pepper said, "We will never let that happen."

Left and Right couldn't believe what they were hearing. They finally had friends who would protect them no matter what.

Towards the end of yet another long day, a young couple and their young daughter walked into the thrift store. Unlike most people, however, they started walking toward the back of the store.

Betty's heart started racing. *Please, please, stop*, she thought. If she had arms, Betty would have waved at them frantically, but they passed the sale rack.

Then, all of a sudden, the mom stopped. "Wait!" she said, backtracking until she was standing in front of Betty and her friends. "Oh, just what I've been looking for! David and Shannon, come see! A big silver bowl, and tossing hands to help make salads with the veggies from our garden. They aren't in perfect condition, but they're perfect for us."

"I think so too, Holly," said David, the dad, who then asked, "What do you think, Shannon?" She nodded, as her dad added, "And I think the salad hands are made out of that beautiful Hawaiian Koa wood." This was music to

Left and Right's ears.

Betty felt so happy for her dream was coming true. But then she heard Salt scream, "You can't leave us in the junk yard!"

Betty's heart broke. Oh no, oh no! she thought, as she was carried, along with Left and Right, to the checkout counter.

Looking back she saw Salt and Pepper waving tearful goodbyes. Will this be the last time we all saw each other? Betty's heart sank.

To everyone's surprise the counter clerk said, "We can give you another discount because these items are damaged."

*NO WE'RE NOT!* thought Betty.

Holly and David quickly looked at each other, and then David said, "Wait, I'll be right back." He rushed off to the sale rack, returning shortly with Salt and Pepper in his hand.

The sale rack friends were together again. The salad hands were clapping with joy, Betty's heart lifted and she had a big smile on her face, and Salt and Pepper were so grateful not to be left behind.

"See, they needed a little spice in their life!" added Salt proudly.

# CHAPTER 6

Leaving the thrift store, the happy family piled into a little red VW Bug, David at the wheel, Holly beside him, and Shannon in the back.

"Sweetheart, why don't you hold our new kitchen utensils on the way home," Holly said, placing Betty, who was now holding Left and Right and Salt and Pepper, in Shannon's lap.

"Mom, it looks like I'm holding a bowl of friends," Shannon said with a big laugh.

Betty felt like she was hugging her brothers and sisters close to her heart. She was dreaming about what their new home would be like and how wonderful the kitchen would be. Kitchens were important to Betty. Poor Salt and Pepper were so exhausted from worrying about being left behind they fell sound asleep next to Left and Right.

Betty was amazed by what she could see out of the car window. *So this is what the world looks like!* The journey from the factory to the store had been scary, bumpy, and dark. *It's hard to see the beauty around you if you're stuffed in a box.*

The clicking sound of the car's turn signal caught Betty's attention. The little red Bug turned onto a country dirt lane, churning up dust and bouncing over potholes. Oh, *I hope we stop here. This little farm would be a dream come true!*

Something bright, silver and round, like Betty but way too big to be a bowl, suddenly caught her eye. *Is it a gigantic toaster?* she wondered.

Betty's dream did come true for this was her new home. Under an ancient oak tree, surrounded by a white picket fence, with rainbow-colored flowers everywhere, stood an old restored Silver Streak trailer.

Betty had never seen anything this big and bright – and silver, just like her. She wondered if it too had been made in a factory. Could she be about to meet a distant relative?

The car stopped in front of the shiny trailer. Everyone slowly piled out of the car after the long day of shopping.

"Shannon, do you need me to carry the bowl?" her mom asked.

"It's okay, Mom, I've got it." As her mom and dad smiled, Shannon picked up Betty and held her close.

*The dream is really coming true!* Betty thought, knowing she and her friends had finally found their forever home. She had no idea that an amazing adventure was about to begin.

# CHAPTER 7

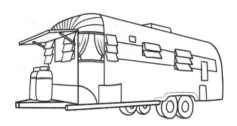

As Shannon carried Betty to the trailer, she thought how different everything was from the old, dark factory where she was born. *I'm so lucky to call this place my home.* She spotted a garden with perfect little rows of vegetables, and a big orchard with fruit trees full of apples, plums, apricots, peaches, and busy beehives. Although she had never seen real, fresh vegetables before, Betty felt that she would spend a lot of time in that beautiful little garden.

"Hey, where are we?" Salt and Pepper, who had just awakened, thought they were dreaming. "Are we camping? Where's the campfire?"

Betty laughed. "Can you believe it, Salt and Pepper? This is our new home sweet home!"

Left and Right were hanging onto Betty's rim to get a good view. In their minds, it all sure looked better than the sale rack.

The vintage Silver Streak was small, but it was everything Betty dreamed her home would be. As everyone made their way through the trailer, she noticed family photos, a big bookshelf full of cookbooks, an old overstuffed couch, and a vase of flowers set on a hand-me-down dining table.

Shannon stepped over the family dog, a big black Labrador wearing a red dog collar with several bright-colored tags and snoring away on the kitchen floor. "Excuse me, Waddlin," Shannon said. She gently placed Betty and her friends on the small counter.

The kitchen was quite small, but that didn't matter to Betty, for it was their kitchen now. It even smelled and looked like a kitchen in which people made real food and cooked from scratch. Old-style kitchen utensils were hanging near the stove, and a cast-iron skillet sat right on it, ready for some home cooking. Betty knew right away she would soon be busy.

Salt and Pepper were delighted when Shannon placed them in the center of the kitchen table, which had been their special place in their first home. Left and Right clapped and signed how happy they were too.

A short time later, Holly walked into the tiny kitchen and told Shannon they would make a big garden salad for dinner. Holly picked up Betty and said, "We will use our beautiful new bowl to bring in a bunch of lettuce and veggies from the garden." Betty felt really special as Left and Right jumped inside her when no one was looking.

"Mom, I'll meet you in the garden," Shannon said. "Come on, Waddlin!" she called to her best friend, and rushed out. She knew exactly where to find the best vegetables to pick for dinner. Waddlin wasn't far behind, her nose to the ground and her tail wagging with excitement.

Holly, ready to follow Shannon, picked up Betty and noticed Left and Right. "Oh, did I put you in the bowl, too?"

20

she wondered aloud. "Huh, I guess I did."

Betty, Left and Right had never felt or smelled garden soil, since today was their first lesson on living in the country.

Holly cut fresh butter lettuce on her hands and knees, remembering all the time she'd spent on her Grandmother Webber's Nebraska farm. Closer to the ground the better, she reminded herself.

Shannon watched her mom's every move as she worked the soil with her bare hands. It looked as if she was having a fun conversation with the chocolate-colored dirt.

Using Left and Right, Shannon busily dug in the dirt for one of her favorite vegetables, "new" potatoes. The potatoes she dug up – brown, yellow, purple and red, some big and some small – reminded Shannon of colored Easter eggs. Digging for them was like an Easter egg hunt, and this was the most fun task in the garden. Shannon shared her mother's and her grandmother's love of the soil and life on a family farm.

Betty was on the ground between everyone in the garden, holding all the freshly harvested lettuces, potatoes, tomatoes, celery, onions, and bell peppers.

Later, as the new family headed back up the worn garden trail, Betty looked forward to her first meal and thought how much fun it would be to sit in the center of the family dinner table.

The dinner – garden salad with fresh-baked rolls spread with butter from a neighbor's Jersey cow – didn't last long. Everyone ate well and until they were happily stuffed. Dishes were cleaned along with Betty, who absolutely loved her first-ever bubble bath.

Later as she was sitting on the counter drying off, an unfamiliar voice came out of nowhere: "The address is 123 Garden Way. It's going to be 75 degrees and sunny tomorrow."

"Who are you? Why are you telling us all this?" Betty asked.

"Oh, I'm a smart phone and I know all kinds of cool stuff. Ask me anything. You can call me Smart. Nice to meet you, Betty."

"You even know my name?" Betty asked, surprised.

"I said I'm smart."

"I know your name, silly," Betty said.

"No, I'm really smart and I can answer any question you have."

"So you know everything?" Betty asked with a little smirk.

"Okay, you asked for it," said Smart. "The bowl was invented in ancient times out of pottery or wood, but in modern times, you are often made out of stainless steel. That's just a very short version of what I know. You don't want me to do a search on bowls because I will never stop talking." Making sure everyone could hear him, Smart barked out, "My kind, on the other hand, is new to the world and our beginning was in the valley 'Silicon'."

"Hmm. Well, that's very interesting and you do know a lot, Smart. I'd love to keep talking to you, but I've had a big day. I can hardly keep my eyes open."

Smart said, "I'm glad we met, Betty. You're nice and I'm excited to have someone to talk to. Good night."

"Good night, Smart. Sweet dreams."

"Oh, I can look that up!"

"NO!" Betty giggled. "Just go to sleep, please!"

# CHAPTER 8

Morning arrived with the rising sun smiling warmly over the countryside. The little silver trailer was quiet as a mouse, except for the new crew in the kitchen. Betty just couldn't stop thinking about fresh homemade pancakes – from scratch, of course. *I remember having pancakes a long time ago. But where and when?*

Salt and Pepper couldn't stop talking about the rooster crowing outside, because he woke them up from their beauty sleep way too early. They didn't know the country woke up to different sounds than in the city, where Salt and Pepper had lived.

Betty assembled the crew and gave them a list of items needed for the surprise pancakes. Everything in the kitchen was easy picking, thanks to Left and Right's handy help. The only things missing were fresh eggs, which were outside in the chicken coop. Not a big problem, except for a really BIG and mean rooster that protected his prized hens and their eggs. He would gladly attack anyone who got between him and his hens. Because Left and Right were the only ones in the crew that could run and grab things, they were quickly elected to collect the eggs — which, as far as the rooster was concerned, meant "stealing."

Suddenly, Left and Right began signing like crazy. "We will only risk going into the chicken coop for Betty, because she is our best friend and that's what friends do. Plus, the pancakes sound so delicious."

Left signed to Right, "Remember we are made from Koa wood and we must be fearless collecting these eggs."

Right signed back, "Don't worry, I'm with you, brother."

After quickly strategizing, the plan was set.

Betty announced, "We need to hurry. We have a lot of mixing and cooking to do before our new family wakes up!"

"But how do we all get out to the chicken coop?" asked Salt and Pepper.

All of a sudden, Betty started spinning and flying around the kitchen, then landed back on the counter with a big smile! I'm such a show off, she thought.

"How did you learn to do that?" everyone asked, their voices full of wonder and awe.

Betty told them that after she was made in the factory, she was moving down the production line so fast that she started spinning and lifted off the moving belt. She never forgot that feeling of freedom. So, at night in the thrift store, while everyone was sleeping, she would fly around the store like a spaceship, having some fun while also practicing her new flying skills.

"Okay, let's go, we're running out of time," Betty announced to the crew.

Left and Right helped Salt and Pepper and Smart into Betty. She flew them all out of the trailer through

Waddlin's dog door, like a shot out of a cannon. Betty had to turn sideways and almost lost everyone! She adjusted her skills to fly with passengers, and couldn't resist flying everyone around for a while, above the trailer and garden for a bird's eye view. Everything looked different and smaller from above.

Smart was wondering out loud if he should turn on his mapping program, but just then Betty made a beeline dive for the chicken coop. Smart looked disappointed – Betty suspected he liked showing off.

Inside the chicken coop, the egg robbers had to move really fast before the rooster spotted them. And if Left and Right had seen how big the rooster was, they wouldn't have braved going into the coop, no matter how much they loved Betty.

Everyone was moving into position when suddenly the rooster crowed. The egg robbers froze in their tracks. After a few seconds, the chicken coop turned quiet again and everyone breathed with relief. *Sitting on the sale rack was way easier than this adventure*, thought Betty, but the others knew how much she wanted to make pancakes for their new family.

Left and Right quietly opened the coop door and climbed in. Left signed, reminding Right that Koa wood stood for courage. But when they looked up, the sleeping rooster was right above them – and he was huge! They inched quietly toward the egg-laying boxes to "borrow" a few eggs. No big deal, no one would miss them, right?

Smart was shining his phone flashlight, when all of a sudden he started ringing! "Oh no!" he hissed. "I forgot to turn myself to silent before I started this mission. I should have been smarter!"

Startled, the rooster and hens started squawking and dashed out of the hen house, giving Right and Left just enough time to collect the eggs and climb back into Betty, who lifted up and away.

Everyone was happy to be heading home with the prized, organic, farm-fresh eggs. Betty was proud of her friends for overcoming their fears to help her with the family breakfast. This time, as she prepared to zoom back through the dog door, everyone held on. Turning sideways and spinning, she zoomed right through and landed in a perfect 10 pose. Not one egg was broken! Mission accomplished! And the egg robbers hadn't even woken up Waddlin, who was still sound asleep, snoring away on her big pillow,

# CHAPTER 9

The breakfast chaos had begun. "Okay, team, let's make an awesome meal!" Betty shouted and gave everyone orders on what to do.

Left and Right had to mix pancake batter, so Smart looked up *Top 10 Pancake Flavors* and found them an easy-to-follow recipe. They began making batter for banana chocolate chip pancakes.

Salt and Pepper were to cook eggs, so Smart found them a how-to YouTube video. Soon Salt and Pepper shook, rattled and rolled over the eggs scrambling in the cast-iron skillet.

Betty watched her crew, hoping her new family would love their wonderful farm-fresh surprise breakfast. In the midst of all stirring, scrambling and commotion, Shannon walked into the kitchen.

Everyone froze and stood quietly, hoping Shannon wouldn't realize what was going on and would go back to bed.

"Can I please lick the spoon?" Shannon asked. Betty was a little surprised that the girl wasn't afraid to see the kitchen utensils come to life.

"What is your name?" Shannon asked, as she happily licked pancake batter from the spoon.

"Oh, you can hear us!" Betty exclaimed. "My name is Betty. Nice to meet you."

"My name is Shannon," she replied with a giggling grin. "Remember we met yesterday? I'm ten next week."

Betty announced, "Hey, everyone, this is our new friend, Shannon."

Salt and Pepper said "Hola!" in unison, and Left and Right went crazy signing. Shannon's eyes grew big with amazement – she had no idea what signing was – so Betty happily explained.

"Wow, that looks like fun," Shannon replied. She tried to sign back, but her fingers quickly became all mixed up.

Smart did a quick search on how to sign, and before long Shannon was able to sign "Hi" back to Left and Right.

Everyone was so happy to have a new friend. Shannon was a big help setting the table and placing fresh garden flowers in a mason jar as the centerpiece.

Before long, everything was ready. Now, Shannon's mom and dad just needed to wake up and join them in the kitchen.

Waddlin was already up as her big nose started to smell the good food made by Betty and the crew. Wadd had an amazing nose and could smell cookies or BBQ from a mile away. She loved having her nose to the ground, smelling all the wonderful scents around the trailer, garden, and, most importantly, the kitchen. *What a great way to start the day!* Waddlin thought.

The smell of coffee brewing must have done its job, because Holly sleepily walked into the kitchen and before long was holding a hot cup of the black stuff. She didn't yet know that Betty and friends, including Shannon, had a wonderful pancake breakfast waiting for her and David.

When Shannon pulled on her mom's PJ sleeve, Holly suddenly saw all the amazing food sitting on the kitchen table. She couldn't believe her eyes. "Look at this! Shannon, you cooked all this wonderful food?"

Shannon and Betty just giggled and grinned, and Shannon said, "Well, I had help, Mom."

Before Holly could say anything, Shannon's dad wandered in, his morning hair in full bed-head bloom. Seeing the kitchen table, he high-fived Holly, but she told him that she didn't make this wonderful breakfast and winked at Shannon, who in turn, winked at Betty.

The sale-rack-egg-robbing crew was so proud they had pulled off the big breakfast surprise for their family. Now it was time to dig into some of the best banana chocolate-chip pancakes and scrambled eggs ever!

After every morsel was eaten and her dad went to get ready for the day, Shannon put Salt and Pepper, Left and Right into Betty, since she wanted to tell her mom who really made the marvelous meal.

"Mom, remember I said I had help in making breakfast?

Holly, who was wiping the counter, said, "Yes, sweetheart?"

"Well, this is Betty," said Shannon, presenting the shiny bowl to her mom. "Left and Right, and Salt and Pepper," she said, pointing them all out. "They made breakfast."

But none of them moved or even said a peep. They all looked just like kitchen utensils.

"Oh," said Holly, who nodded. "I understand, sweetheart. I had magical friends when I was young, too."

29

And as Holly went back to wiping the counter, Shannon sighed and then smiled, thinking, *Boy, Mom is really going to be surprised someday.*

# CHAPTER 10

Shannon and her mom were on kitchen detail. They cleaned up, and tucked Betty and her friends away in different parts of the kitchen.

As the cleanup was underway, Betty overheard Shannon's mom and dad talking about heading off to the local farmers' market.

"Smart, what's a farmers' market?" Betty whispered.

Smart whispered back, "That's easy, check this out." His screen immediately lit up, and Betty read: *Farmers' markets* may be indoors or outdoors and typically consist of booths, tables or stands where *farmers* sell fruits, vegetables, meats, cheeses, and sometimes prepared foods and beverages. *Farmers' markets* exist in many countries worldwide and reflect the *local* culture and economy.

"Wow," Betty said. "I would love to go to a farmers' market and meet some of the farmers – though I guess they might not know how to talk to a silver bowl. And I know Left and Right and Salt and Pepper would love to go, too."

Betty's conversation came to an abrupt end when David picked up Smart and herded Holly and Shannon out the door to the little red Bug.

Left and Right quickly grabbed Salt and Pepper, climbed into Betty and took off out the dog door, catching up with the Bug as it headed down the driveway in a cloud of dust.

As Betty and her crew flew along above the Bug, the countryside resembled a huge patchwork of well-manicured gardens. It went on as far as you could see, until it blended into the horizon. The little red car looked like a ladybug. They could see Shannon looking up and waving at them from the back seat.

Suddenly the sky turned dark, and the wind began to toss Betty around like she was on a wild rollercoaster ride. A big flash of lighting sliced through the sky like a sharp knife, nearly cutting Betty in two. A deafening crack of thunder followed. Salt and Pepper started screaming in Spanish, saying even the chicken coop was much safer than this crazy ride. Right and Left were shaking and clinging on for dear life. Betty needed to do something quickly, so she swooped down until she was flying in calmer air, closer to the Bug -- and to her new human family.

As the wild rollercoaster ride ended, Left and Right signed a big thank you to Betty for saving everyone's lives. Salt and Pepper finally caught their breath and said at the exact same time, "Can we all please ride home in the Bug with Shannon?"

Betty thought, *That's the best idea I've heard all day!*

As they cruised along, a funny honking sound echoed around them. *What's that noise?* wondered Betty, hoping it wasn't the beginning of another stormy ride.

Then they spotted an entire flock of geese just above them in a perfect V formation. They had never seen geese before. The birds had probably flown thousands of miles from their winter home, and were headed south for warmer weather.

Betty and her crew would have loved flying with the geese, but they had a schedule to meet. So they all waved goodbye, hoping to meet the geese again someday.

Before long, Betty spotted a small town below. The little red Bug pulled into a parking area near an area where people were busy setting up their booths for the farmers' market.

Getting out of the Bug, Shannon heard a familiar sound and looked up to see Betty hovering above. She was excited and relieved her new friends had found their way here. "You made it!" she yelled, amazed they had flown through the thunder and lightning. "Just follow me!"

Shannon hurried after her parents into the market. Wandering around farmers' markets was one of Shannon's favorite ways to spend Saturdays. It reminded her of the country fair that came around once a year, but she could visit the farmers' market every week. The farmers were so nice, and always gave her samples of seasonal fruits and vegetables. Holly reminded Shannon that food grown and produced nearby was always best, because it was fresher, and a lot of resources weren't wasted shipping food from far away.

"Farmer Shu!" Shannon said loudly, spotting one of her favorite farmers.

"Hi, Shannon! I have some of your favorite baby carrots and my super sweet strawberries."

"Thank you," Shannon said, cupping the baby carrots in her hands. *This is more fun than Halloween*, she thought. She loved strawberries too, and remembered a funny little fact that they were the only fruit known to have seeds on the outside of their skin.

As the family happily wove their way through the market crowd, they could smell the most delicious scent in the air – it was coming from the fresh-baked bread booth. The little old baker saw his young friend hurrying over, walking much faster than her parents. He was ready to make her day.

As he always did, the baker handed Shannon a slice of warm bread, spread with country butter and topped with fresh strawberry jam. This was a slice of heaven!

She finished the wonderful bread just as her mom appeared at her side.

"Mom, can I please have another slice?"

"Shannon, your eyes are bigger than your stomach! We're only halfway through the market, and you know your other farmer friends will want to give you samples of their harvest too."

Shannon pushed out her tummy and her mom laughed out loud.

Part of the day's fun for Shannon was discovering new vegetables she'd never seen before. Today one farmer showed her an unusually round, lumpy celery root quite unlike the smooth green celery stalks she enjoyed with her mom's home-ground peanut butter. Another showed her heirloom tomatoes, which were really odd looking with their bulbous shapes and variety of artful colors, but tasted as sweet as candy.

Betty and friends hovered above, watching Shannon as she wandered from stall to stall. Betty enjoyed seeing how a farmers' market worked; it reminded her of watching the good vibe of a busy beehive.

After a while, the reusable bags Shannon and her parents carried couldn't hold even one more sweet potato. It was time to head home. They stuffed everything into the little red Bug and off they went, bouncing down the small-town road with country music on the radio, the windows down, and fresh sweet air blowing in their faces. Everyone had enjoyed today's farmers' market.

Shannon had fallen sound asleep to the serenade of the Bug's little engine. She was dreaming of all the fun food at the farmers' market, and her birthday party next week.

High above, her friends flew past to arrive home before Shannon and her parents. Swooping down out of the clear blue sky, Betty yelled "Hold on!" and dove right through the trees and aimed for the dog door at the end of the porch.

Waddlin was curled up in the last sunny spot on the kitchen floor. She heard the crash landing and looked up. Since no food was hitting the floor and the new friends were back home safe and sound, she gladly went back to sleep.

Betty knew the red Bug would be heading up the driveway soon. "To your places, crew!" she said, and everyone tumbled out of her and arranged themselves in the kitchen.

Soon, Shannon and her parents arrived, and before long the tiny kitchen counter began to look like the crowded farmers' market. Beautiful fruits and vegetables were stacked everywhere. When no one was looking, Shannon snuck a juicy apple out of its basket and took a big bite. *So sweet and delicious, God's candy*, she thought.

Betty saw the apple heist, but Shannon put a finger to her lips: *Please don't tell!* They both giggled and smiled, knowing they shared a secret that was theirs alone.

Everybody wanted to help organize the day's purchases. The kitchen became like a dance floor with everyone moving in rhythm, working together. Not a word was spoken, for they all knew the dance steps to this wonderful unwritten kitchen song.

The family decided that twice-baked stuffed potatoes and a big garden salad would be on the menu tonight. That sounded great to Betty and her crew, for tonight they would prepare their first dinner together in their new kitchen.

Smart was ready with directions on the best way to bake russet potatoes, which are also known as "bakers." They needed a little bath with olive oil, freshly ground sea salt, and then into the oven they went.

Shannon and Betty teamed up to select veggies from today's farmers' market and from their home garden, and created a big chopped salad. Just about anything and everything, including leftovers, could be used. Shannon couldn't wait to show Mom and Dad their creation, which would be known forever as the "MONSTER SALAD."

Shannon loved dinners outside on the porch, with the sun saying good night and the fireflies appearing like tiny stars dancing to the music of the crickets.

After a farm-to-table family dinner, Betty and the other dishes were washed, and Betty was put in her place of honor on the kitchen counter, holding the day's beautiful fresh bounty.

The entire family, over-stuffed like the baked potatoes they'd just enjoyed, happily went off to bed, thinking, *Early to bed and early to rise.*

# CHAPTER 11

Time really flies by for a kid in the country with farm chores, school, hanging out with friends, homework, keeping your room clean, taking care of your best friend who happens to be a dog, and keeping a big rooster from attacking you.

And before she knew it, Shannon's birthday had arrived.

It's hard to sleep in on the day of your birthday. As soon as the sun worked its way up over the hill, like fresh bread dough slowly rising, Shannon was wide awake and thinking about all the fun she was going to have. Today she turned ten, and being double digits is a BIG deal. Shannon could not believe that in only three years, she would be a TEEN!

In the kitchen, it was busy as a beehive again, and Betty was the queen bee. She couldn't wait to make this a special day for Shannon. It started early, with Betty and Smart researching French toast recipes on the Internet, and Left and Right busy collecting all the ingredients needed for the day's special meal.

The crew knew Shannon and Waddlin would be

showing up soon for breakfast. Smart could almost set his clock by the arrival of a hungry Shannon with her doggy shadow at her side, since Waddlin's job was to make sure the floor was cleaned up before Shannon's mom or dad arrived on the scene. The kitchen was now the first morning stop for Shannon because she knew Betty would be cooking. This made Betty very proud. Cooking with friends and for friends. *Life just couldn't get any better!*

Shannon had always been an early riser, and Saturday was her day to roam the little farm. Sharing the sunrise and the quiet sounds of morning with Waddlin was special and they both loved their time together. "Come on Waddlin, let's get scadaddlin'!" The garden at this time was still asleep, but as soon as the sun rose and broke the darkness, the garden woke up and reached out for warmth. Waddlin always had her nose to the ground and Shannon was never far behind. It was as if Waddlin was in a world of her own and Shannon was just along for the ride. Sometimes Shannon did wish Waddlin could talk, but they had an unspoken language that spoke to their hearts.

Before heading back to the house, Shannon asked Waddlin, "Have you seen any more snails?" When Waddlin stopped in her tracks, tail wagging madly, Shannon knew the signal. She bent down near Waddlin's nose, picked up a snail and put it in a small tin can. "Good job, girl, you found a big one!" Shannon said, and patted Waddlin on the head.

By now the can was nearly full and the hens were all lined up waiting for their morning treats. Shannon's mom paid her fifty cents per can for her pest control on the farm. Her parents didn't like using harmful chemicals, so collecting snails was a fun and organic way to earn extra allowance money.

As Shannon and Waddlin walked the worn path back to the trailer, between the two worlds they loved, garden and home, the smell of French toast was in the air. Their pace picked up to a full run. The race was on, snails and all!

As Shannon and Waddlin crossed the imaginary finish line to the trailer door, Shannon knew Betty's French toast was waiting for her. It was the first-place prize for winning the race. Mom and Dad were still asleep, as was usual for the weekend, and this gave Shannon first dibs on the French toast. Sliding into the kitchen in her big socks, having left her mud-crud boots outside, she yelled, "Hey, guys, I have a fresh can of snails. Anybody want some?"

Salt and Pepper cried out, "Gross! No gracias."

Of course Smart then announced, "Snails are considered a delicacy in many countries and are called escargot."

Salt and Pepper shot back, "Who cares – it's still gross!"

Shannon laughed, since she kind of agreed with Salt and Pepper.

As Shannon turned to Betty, she found perched on the kitchen counter a big, beautiful birthday cake adorned with strawberries, peaks of whipped cream, and white chocolate curlicues.

"Who ...? When ...? How ...?" she exclaimed — but she realized right away who had made the wonderful cake. "Ahh, you guys!" she said, and secretly hummed, "Think I'll try a little of the frosting to make sure it tastes okay." But a little voice inside said, *Not a good idea, my friend*, so Shannon didn't steal a taste.

The next gift of the day was raisin bread French toast, eggs, and fresh-squeezed orange juice. "You guys are the best!" Shannon yelled out.

The crew smiled with delight as everyone thought, *So much better to give than to receive!*

# CHAPTER 12

Shannon's tenth birthday party was going to be in her all-time favorite park, and she was busy organizing her backpack for the day. *Wow, I'm really ten today,* she thought, thinking too about how life was changing all around her. Instinctively, Shannon knew things wouldn't be the same as when she was nine years old. *I guess this is what they call growing up. I'm not afraid at all.*

Just like the young birds on their farm, little by little she had been testing her wings without really thinking about it. She rode her bike further down the road as her neighborhood seemed much smaller now. At school she looked forward to her geography class, reading and learning about faraway places she wanted to visit someday. And she listened more to that little voice inside that always gave good advice.

Suddenly Waddlin ran into her room, pulling Shannon away from her daydreaming. "Okay, Wadd, I'm coming." She grabbed her back pack and rushed to the car thinking about her birthdays in the past, particularly the year when a very special gift was a little black puppy she named

Shadow ... who always waddled.

All Shannon's best friends from school, and their dogs, were invited to this year's party. Waddlin wasn't too happy about this, because it meant big competition for any food that found its way to the ground.

"Let's go, Shannon!" Mom called out. It was finally time to load all the party goods into the little red Bug, including Betty, Smart, Left and Right, and Salt and Pepper. Betty asked Smart to send Holly a text telling her not to forget them! Also stuffed into the Bug was the food, one big black dog, and the be-au-tiful birthday cake. Everyone and everything was packed in like kernels on a summer ear of corn. Today Betty had the honor of holding the huge fresh salad Holly made with lettuce Shannon had picked just for her birthday. Left and Right were happy to toss, and Salt and Pepper were ready to "Shake it, baby!" As always, Smart was in charge of technology and would be snapping photos of Shannon's tenth birthday to add to the family's growing digital album.

Off they went for the quick drive to the park. Her parents chatted while Shannon thought she could have beaten the Bug to the park by riding her bike on a path she made with her good buddy Joe. The neighborhood kids developed a secret network of paths that connected the whole community, and had become experts on those hidden bike highways.

In the park, four large picnic benches were reserved for Shannon's big party. Her dad had stopped by earlier in the day and placed old family tablecloths over each bench to secure the spot. It looked like a tapestry of family colors and history. The tablecloths had been handed down by relatives who would be attending Shannon's tenth birthday party in spirit. Some she remembered vaguely and others she only knew by looking at old black-and-white family photos, which made her feel connected to her family's past. When she held the photo of her great-grandma, Shannon felt she was holding her hand.

Today's party was potluck style. Shannon loved this type of party, where everyone brought food from their kitchens made from hand-me-down recipes like the hand-me-down quilted tablecloths. *Buffet style and all you can eat*, Shannon thought with a smile.

David was proudly elected the BBQ master, just like his dad had been back in the day, and Smart was elected to be the party DJ as well as photographer. He was so excited when he saw the big speakers. There was even a dance floor, and Smart already had a list of songs to play.

That morning, down the road and across the street, Joe had woken up early, too. He sensed something was different as he sat up in bed, and then he remembered it was Shannon's birthday! His girlfriend was going to be ten today! (In Joe's mind, Shannon was his girl, but they were actually just good friends.)

Joe couldn't wait to wear his new Vans sneakers to Shannon's party. He'd thought about wearing them to bed the night before the party to help break them in. But no! As he laced them up now, he laughed, thinking how his Vans would've looked with his PJs.

Dressed and ready to go, Joe made an important stop before going downstairs. He checked, found the coast was clear, and headed into his mom and dad's bathroom. Joe opened a cabinet next to the sink, where his dad kept all his manly stuff. Joe knew his mom could walk by the bathroom any minute, so he had to hurry.

He found what he needed: his dad's aftershave. This would be the icing on the cake. He'd seen all the aftershave commercials on TV during football games and knew that, along with the Vans, this was all he needed to impress Shannon.

"Joe! We've got to get going or you'll be late for Shannon's birthday party," his mom called up from downstairs. "You told her dad you'd help with the BBQ, right?"

"Okay, I'm coming," Joe said, putting the aftershave back in the exact same spot and leaving no evidence of tampering. Then he was down the stairs and in the car like a shot.

When he climbed in, his mom, who was already at the wheel, sniffed and said, "Holy cow, I've got to talk to Dad. This car smells like a whole bottle of aftershave."

Joe just kept looking out the window, hoping the moment would pass.

"Well, don't you look handsome today?"

"Thanks, Mom," Joe replied, checking out his new Vans and hoping Shannon would think he looked handsome, too.

"Joe, what did you get Shannon for her birthday?" his mom asked as she backed the car down the long driveway. This always made her nervous because she had run over the mailbox a few times. Joe was ready for a crash at any second, and was pretty sure he could back up the car better than his mom.

"I bought Shannon a pound of organic gummy bears, Mom. Do you think she'll like them?"

"Oh, for sure, Joe. It's a nice thought and organic is good for our planet."

Organic always cost a little more, but Joe thought Shannon was worth the extra allowance money he had earned by washing his parents' cars.

Things were going great until their car turned into the parking lot, rolled over a curb, and almost pushed a big trashcan over. The girls on the dance floor paused and looked over; all eyes were on Joe as he groaned and sunk down into his seat.

All he could say, in a quiet voice, was, "Bye, Mom."

"Joe, are you okay?" she asked.

He grabbed the birthday-wrapped gummy bears and off he went.

"Bye, Joe, have fun!" was the last he heard as he left the safety of the family car, gripping the gummy bears and tripping over his squeaky new Vans.

"Hey, Joe!"

"Hi, Mr. Peterson," Joe said.

"Glad you're here. I need your help at the BBQ!" David yelled.

Happy to be out of the spotlight, Joe's fear disappeared as quickly as it arrived and he joined Shannon's dad near the BBQ. David had placed an upside-down milk crate near it so Joe could reach the grill. Joe also had his very own apron and BBQ baseball cap. This was so much better than dancing with the girls.

"Joe, I didn't know you were shaving now," David remarked. "A little heavy on the aftershave, don't you think?"

After everyone ate their fill of amazing BBQ and the delicious side dishes, Shannon blew out the ten candles on her be-au-tiful strawberry cake. Now it was time for the presents. But instead of wrapped gifts, a big bunch of envelopes waited for Shannon, which made her smile.

Shannon knew it always felt better to give than to receive. From a very early age, she loved helping people, opening a door for an elderly person or helping one of her fellow students with a school project they were struggling with. And her room in the little silver trailer was so small she just didn't need any more *stuff*. For this birthday, she had asked her friends to "gift" her with ideas for a project that would help people in need in their community. As the birthday girl, she would pick her favorite idea and present it to their teacher at school. Parents had gladly donated a little money to finance a project..

Everyone gathered around as Shannon opened each envelope and read the ideas out loud to her birthday guests. After she finished, she knew right away which project she would pick. She thanked her school buddies and announced she had picked her friend Kit's project. Everyone applauded as Shannon gave Kit a big hug. Kit's idea was to start a school glass and aluminum recycling drive. Money raised would be used to build a community-style garden and a cooking-from-scratch lunch program at their school.

As the day wound down, Mom said, "Okay, Shannon, it's time to start saying goodbye to everyone. Let's get a wiggle on!"

"Okay, Mom," Shannon said, but the school garden and lunch program were still fresh on her mind. *I know Betty and the crew would love working in the cafeteria, and I can drop them off at the kitchen in the morning before my first class.*

As everyone started to leave, food was wrapped up for leftovers so nothing would go to waste. Betty, along with other pots and pans, was stacked on one of the benches near the BBQ. It was a big stack and Betty was near the bottom. She could see that people were leaving and didn't have a good feeling about her predicament. She was stacked with pans she did not know.

Left and Right were signing, "Where's Betty?" Smart was in David's pocket and out of sight, so he couldn't help. Salt and Pepper were trying their best to get Shannon's attention, but everyone was so busy saying their goodbyes that no one heard them.

*They wouldn't leave me behind*, Betty thought, just as the little red Bug started the journey back home ... without her! *Oh dear, this is not good.*

Betty tried with all her might to spin free of the stack, but too much weight held her down. She hoped that when her family arrived home, someone would notice she wasn't there. She knew in her heart Shannon would be back as soon as she realized Betty had been left in the park.

Time passed like cold honey on a spoon as Betty tried to keep up her spirits. She remembered how some people had said she wasn't a perfect bowl because of her little dent, but Betty knew better. She remembered sitting on that sale rack for what seemed like forever, but her patience and optimism kept her spirits up. And one day, just as she'd hoped, the right family had come along and loved her.

Not too far from where Betty was trapped, another party was ending. This wasn't a birthday party, and everyone was much older than Shannon and her friends. As they walked past where Betty was helplessly stranded, one of the guests said, "Well, well. I could use these pans in my kitchen."

A voice behind him called, "William, those pans don't belong to you! Leave them alone!"

"Too bad," William hissed back like a snake. "They're mine now, and I'll do what I want with them." He stood by the stack of pans like a guard at his post, waiting for his friend to leave the park so he could pack up the goods and steal them.

Betty was already thinking she didn't like this guy, but she was helpless, as were the other captives. Soon she was again shoved in a dark box, and bounced around in the back of a van, with no idea where she was headed.

Where is Shannon? Is she looking for me?

Oh, how she missed everyone already, even the rooster. *Well, maybe not the rooster.* But this time Betty wasn't as afraid, because she knew Shannon and her friends would come looking for her.

# CHAPTER 13

The little red Bug bounced down the road on the way home as everyone except David, who was driving, and Shannon, who was thinking about her wonderful birthday, fell asleep. By now it was way past bedtime and all the food and fun and excitement they'd had that day made everyone sleepy.

When the family reached the little silver trailer, David and Shannon said, "We're home!" together, and were the first out of the car.

"Dad, I'm so tired, I can't take another step," Shannon announced.

"What?" David said with a big smile. "Come on – you're ten now!"

Shannon gave her dad "the look."

"Okay," said David. "How about a piggy back ride to the house?" He bent down and she jumped on his back. "Wow, you're so heavy, Shannon. It must have been all the cake you ate!" They both laughed, and Dad took off up to the house with Shannon aboard.

Shannon hugged her dad when she jumped off,

thinking how lucky she was. She thanked God for such a wonderful father, and friend too.

Waddlin had had a long day, too. Having to compete for wayward nibbles with the other party dogs wore her out. After a quick visit to her water bowl, she was back to her comfy bed and soon happily sound asleep.

However, when Salt and Pepper and Left and Right woke up from the car ride, they looked around and realized something ... something awful. *Betty wasn't there! She hadn't made it home in the car! They needed to do something – now!*

"Quick," said Salt. "Emergency meeting to figure out what to do! Smart, we need you thinking hard!"

Mom picked everyone up and brought them into the kitchen, but when she picked up Smart and headed for the couch, the rest of the crew realized *"now!"* would have to wait. Mom plopped down next to David on the couch, and they began to look at the photos of Shannon's party that Smart had taken that afternoon.

"Oh, no," signed Left and Right. "We need Smart to help us figure out what to do about Betty."

"Let's sleep on it," said Pepper.

"I guess we'll have to," said Salt. "Smart is the brains in the family, and who knows how long he'll be stuck showing his photos."

Morning finally came, and Shannon was looking for Waddlin to start their chores. Running by the kitchen, she hit the brakes. Something important was missing. *Betty!* Where was Betty? Perhaps she was in one of the kitchen cabinets. Shannon checked all of them, but Betty was

51

nowhere.

Shannon raced outside, first checking if Betty was stuck in the red Bug, and then covering almost every inch of the little farm. She even checked in the chicken coop, and was relieved Betty wasn't being held hostage by the rooster, although she'd have gladly taken him on to save Betty.

When she returned to the kitchen, upset, she saw the rest of the crew in panic mode talking over each other. Since Salt and Pepper were the loudest, Shannon picked them up and put them in the cookie jar. Oh, they were not happy about that. But Shannon knew the morning was quickly getting out of control. As she turned to speak with Smart, Left and Right started signing like crazy. So at the top of her lungs, Shannon yelled, "Everyone stop! Please!"

Suddenly the kitchen turned as quiet as a church. It was usually such a happy place in the morning, with the group of friends cooking amazing food and planning the day, but this morning it was different, and sad.

*This must be a bad dream*, thought Shannon. But it wasn't. She took Salt and Pepper out of the cookie jar and set them next to Left and Right. By then everyone got the message and focused on Shannon and what she was going to say next.

With hands on hips she said, "We are a family and it's up to us to find Betty. You know that if any of you were lost, I wouldn't stop until I found you. That's what we all have to do for Betty. Are you with me, guys?"

"YES!" everyone cried out.

"Smart, what are you thinking? We need your help!"

"Well, that's what I do best."

"Smart, we know that. Just get to the point, please."

Smart was waiting for this moment. He had done his research and was ready to share his ideas with Shannon and the crew. He switched to HIGH volume and finally got everyone's attention. "My first thought was to go through all the photos I took at the party. I was looking for a suspect that might have an interest in a stainless-steel mixing bowl."

Salt and Pepper chimed in, jokingly asking, "Like a chef?"

"Exactly!"

"Oh, we were just kidding."

Shannon said, "This is not a time to be joking around; we are running out of time!"

"Sorry," said Salt and Pepper.

"No worries," said Smart. "Listen up. There's an app – a face-recognition one that can track and identify faces in a crowd. That's how I found the chef who I think kidnapped Betty. He was in the background of many of the photos. I also know the name of the restaurant he works at – Bill's Diner."

"No way! How did you figure that out?" asked Shannon.

"It's embroidered on his chef's jacket," said Smart.

"That's so clever!" Shannon shouted. Instantly Smart's screen lit up with a smiley face, and Shannon knew her little friend loved the compliment.

"Can I see some of the photos?" she asked.

"Sure, Shannon. Take a look at my screen." Smart scrolled through the photos.

"Wait, Smart – can you go back to the last photo?"

"Yep, here it is."

Amazed, Shannon said, "Take a look at the wicked tattoo on his arm – that is so scary!" But she knew this piece of evidence could help her locate Betty.

"Thank you, Smart."

"You're welcome. I've also mapped out the location and I know exactly where the restaurant is, downtown in the big city."

Everyone looked at each other with a hint of fear on their faces. They had heard about the city, and saw the skyline as Betty was flying them to the farmers' market. It looked big, and very different to the farmland around their home in the country. All except Left and Right let out a big, worried sigh. Smart knew he had to step in and reassure his friends that he had a solid rescue plan.

"It's okay, no big deal. I have a built-in GPS system, and I can get us anywhere in the world."

Wow, everyone thought.

Smart continued, "GPS, which stands for Global Positioning System, is a radio navigation system that allows land, sea, and airborne users to determine their exact location, velocity, and time twenty-four hours a day, in all weather conditions, anywhere in the world."

A groggy, yawning Mom appeared behind Shannon. "What are you doing in the kitchen, sweetheart?" she asked as she made her way to the coffee pot, filled her travel mug, and tossed Smart into her backpack. "It's the weekend and you have chores to do, remember?"

"I was, uh, just getting ... some water," Shannon said. She grabbed a glass, filled it with water, and gulped it down. "Doing chores makes me thirsty," she added.

"Okay, well, your dad and I have to go into town to do some shopping, and we'll probably stop for lunch there, so Norma will stop in and check on you later. Oooh, and maybe she'll leave a little of her homemade cheese in our refrigerator," she added with a grin.

"Great," said Shannon, as she eyed her mom's backpack. A plan was already hatching in her mind on how to get Smart back before her parents left for the day. Because without Smart, they'd never figure out a way to find Betty.

# CHAPTER 14

Shannon waited for the right moment, which came when her dad went out to the car and her mom was still rushing around in the trailer. Mom suddenly dropped her backpack on the couch, saying, "I left my hoodie on our bed. I'll be right back."

Shannon made her move, grabbing Smart out of the backpack and slipping out the side door of the trailer with Waddlin bringing up the rear. Shannon heard her mom running out the door, yelling, "Bye, sweetie, and make sure you get the chores done!"

Shannon waited until the little red Bug rolled down the driveway and turned right onto the highway. When it disappeared from view, she said, "Yes!" Now she had to gather the team – there was no time to spare.

But seconds later, the Bug was headed back up the driveway. "Oh, no," Shannon whispered, thinking her parents were coming back to look for Smart. Figuring it was best if her parents found her in the house and doing a chore, she hurried back into the kitchen, and was washing her water glass when her mom walked in.

"We forgot our reusable grocery bags, sweetheart," Mom said, grabbing the bags and adding, "Be good, see you later," as she again ran out the door.

Shannon sighed with relief, but Left and Right signed, reminding her that the clock was ticking.

"Okay, we don't have a lot of time."

"Shannon," Smart said, "your boyfriend Joe down the street ..."

"Joe is not my boyfriend. He's only eight! Sheesh, he's like my little brother."

"Okay, okay, your friend Joe has a drone with a camera and we will need that to help us find Betty."

Shannon thought how to ask Joe about borrowing his new drone, but came up blank. "I'll find Joe," she said, knowing she'd have to think of something. She ran out of the trailer towards Joe's house.

She made it in record time.

"Hi, Shannon!" said Joe, opening the front door.

"Joe! You've got to help me, please. I need to borrow your new drone," Shannon said quickly. "Sorry, I don't have time to explain – it's an emergency." *Wow, she thought, I said it and Joe didn't slam the door.*

"Hold on!" said Joe. He disappeared but returned seconds later carrying the drone. He handed it over without a word. Shannon was surprised, and so grateful that she gave Joe a kiss on the cheek. He looked like he was about to faint on the spot.

Shannon ran back home as fast as she could. Even Smart was impressed with how fast she made it back with the drone. "Did you kiss Joe for it?" he asked.

Shannon didn't say anything, but she turned bright red. When Salt and Pepper asked when the wedding was,

Shannon reminded them that the cookie jar was within reach.

Then Smart yelled, "We only have a few minutes before the bus arrives at the end of the street. It's the only bus on Sunday to downtown. We have to hurry!"

Remembering one last detail, Shannon quickly wrote a note to Norma: *Change of plans. I'm with my mom and dad. Love, Shannon*. As she taped it to the door, her heart was a little heavy, knowing she wasn't being honest. But rescuing Betty was more important, so she continued with her plan.

Shannon would learn a big lesson today. When you don't tell the truth you must remember everything you say – and that makes life very complicated.

Noticing the looks on everyone's faces, Shannon said, "I'm a little scared too. I've never been to the city or been on the bus to downtown. But we can do this together. We are Betty's 'Rescue Squad', right?"

Everyone shouted or signed, "Yeah! We're the Rescue Squad!" Waddlin barked in agreement.

Shannon stuffed Left and Right, and Salt and Pepper into Waddlin's own doggy backpack, along with some leftover gummy bears, and they left the trailer. Outside, Smart reminded Shannon that she needed to tie him onto the drone with a rubber band. Shannon did that quickly and the drone lifted off and hovered over the team. *Wow, Smart is so smart!* Shannon thought, but then the drone and Smart almost hit a tree branch. Shannon laughed for the first time that day, but Smart did not think it was funny. He got the drone back into hovering position above everyone, and off they went, running and hovering down the street to meet the bus.

The Rescue Squad made it to the corner in a flash, while Smart was still trying to figure out exactly how to fly the drone. He almost crashed into a telephone pole. Then he almost hit the stop sign at the corner where the bus pulled up. At the very last moment, Smart maneuvered the drone sideways, like a fighter jet in a dogfight. Seeing the bus door open, Smart and the drone went right through it and out an open window on the other side of the bus.

Ms. Weasel, the startled bus driver, ducked and hit her head on the steering wheel.

This is not good! Shannon thought, for every child in the valley feared Ms. Weasel. She used to drive the school bus, and Shannon had enough bad memories of that. Ms. Weasel did not like surprises on her bus, and had the personality of a cactus – prickly, to say the least.

As Shannon got ready to board, she asked politely, "Is this the bus to downtown?"

Without looking at Shannon, Ms. Weasel snarled, "Can't you read the sign?"

Shannon could hear Waddlin growling and nudged her to stop it. They didn't need to give Ms. Weasel any other reasons to slam the door shut and drive off. This was the only way to get to downtown today.

Salt and Pepper were asking why it was taking so long to board the bus when Smart landed the drone on the bus roof. Oh no, this is starting to get a little complicated Shannon thought.

Ms. Weasel looked up at the sound, but then barked, "What are you waiting for, young lady? Swipe your bus pass and get on this bus!"

Shannon did not have a bus pass, and she didn't know what to do next. For the first time Ms. Weasel looked down at Shannon. "My bus has to stay on schedule and, by the way, NO dogs allowed," she said, smiling as if enjoying this test of wills. But Shannon was determined to outwit her.

"All I have is this five dollars, and I really need to get to downtown this morning."

Ms. Weasel grabbed the money out of Shannon's hand. "Get on the bus, sit down, be quiet, and make sure that dog is too." The five-dollar bill quickly disappeared and the bus began rolling down the road. Shannon was happy that she had not only stood up to Ms. Weasel, she also hadn't told her that she had two five-dollar bills.

As the drone went zooming by, fueling Shannon's determination to find Betty, she thought, Game On!

# CHAPTER 15

The bus ride was shorter than Shannon expected. Before long the green hills and farm fields disappeared, replaced by concrete, steel, and glass. As the bus made its scheduled stops, people got on and off the bus like robots, not looking up from their morning papers or mobile phones at all, not a hello or smile from anyone.

For Shannon, today was a great adventure. She wasn't heading to school or doing her chores, but was on her way to the BIG city. She was the youngest person on the bus but was feeling quite grown up. Looking out the window, the world before her looked big, exciting, and a little confusing. She was reassured to see Smart hovering nearby, following the bus. Shannon was also happy eating her gummy bears with no one looking over her shoulder and reminding her not to eat too many. The day was turning out to be truly a taste of freedom.

That freedom and security ended when the bus door swung open and Ms. Weasel reminded Shannon, with a harsh look, this was where she needed to get off. For Shannon, and Waddlin too, it was a giant first step into an unknown world.

In her first few seconds of city life, Shannon received a face-full of black bus exhaust, complements of Ms. Weasel. As the bus sped off to its next stop, Shannon could see Ms. Weasel's grin in the bus's large rearview mirror.

Brave as Shannon was, she was not quite ready for the big city.

She found herself in the middle of a wave of people hurrying all around her, in every direction. Waddlin looked up at her with concern, as if to say, *What have you gotten me into?* Shannon patted Wadd on the head and reassured her, "Don't worry, Waddlin, we're in this together. Stay close to me, okay?" She had to quickly step away from the human stampede to plan the Rescue Squad's next move. She was a little frightened at first, but thinking of Betty gave her courage.

Through the chaotic city noises, Shannon heard a buzzing sound. She looked up and was relieved to see Smart landing the drone right next to her.

"Hey, Shannon," Smart barked out over the city noise. "Just like the Mars rover landing!" Everyone else was a bit anxious, but not Smart. For him, this was a dream come true and his rescue plan was on track!

Shannon looked around and spotted an alley just a few steps away. She thought it would be the safest place to get out of the flow of human traffic for a moment. She grabbed the drone, hurried to the alley, and stopped near some trash cans.

Instantly, Salt and Pepper began to complain about the terrible smell.

Suddenly, a voice rang out. "What do you mean, this place smells? This is my home, I live here! I do my best, you know!"

62

The crew looked around and saw a huge rat. At first they wanted to run, but this rat had a big smile and a gold "R" engraved on his front tooth.

Shannon quickly said, "I am sorry that we criticized your home, sir."

"Thank you, and apology accepted," the big rat said. "Now I'm actually glad you stopped by. My name is Raymundo and I don't get many visitors. Yes, my alley does smell a little because of all the wasted food that gets tossed out. It's just not right, with so many hungry people in this city."

Shannon said, "Raymundo, my mom always tells me to not put more on my plate than I can eat."

Raymundo smiled in agreement.

This all reminded Shannon that too many people go to bed hungry every night. She was thankful they ran into Raymundo, and thought someday she would do something about all the wasted food in the world. No one should ever go to bed hungry.

Shannon said goodbye and thanked Raymundo for letting the Rescue Squad get out of harm's way, then reminded everyone it was time to get moving. Smart looked up their position on his GPS app and announced they were just a few blocks away from where he thought Betty was being held captive.

"Okay, here is what we are going to do," Smart said. "I need a set of hands just in case we have to pry open a window or door and sneak into Bill's Diner."

Hearing that, Left and Right unzipped Waddlin's backpack, signed that they were ready to help, and jumped onto the drone with Smart – they had no idea what they were getting themselves into.

At Captain Smart's order, the drone lifted up and shot out of the alley like a rocket, with Shannon and Waddlin running after it. Left and Right held on for dear life as the drone picked up speed and wove its way through the tall buildings of steel and glass. Shannon saw the drone's reflection on building windows, and thought it looked just like a giant dragonfly.

Smart was having the time of his life, until his low-battery buzzer sounded. *Darn it, I'm smarter than that!* Smart thought, realizing he had forgotten to have Shannon recharge him before they ventured off on the rescue mission.

Down below, navigating through a stampede of humanity, the other half of the Rescue Squad had just crossed the street. Shannon thought how different the big cement sidewalks were compared to the dirt trails she and Waddlin wandered on back home.

Shannon held tight onto Wadd, who pulled her through the wind and mass of people going each way. Still determined to find Betty and get everyone back home safely, Shannon knew she would be in big trouble if her parents arrived home first and learned she had taken their phone and gone into the city. And they might find the note she'd left for Norma. She let out a big sigh and told Waddlin, "We have to hurry up big time – we can't let Mom and Dad beat us home."

Waddlin put her nose to the ground and led the way. Shannon looked up and began to laugh when she saw where they were headed – right towards a group of food trucks. Waddlin's nose had picked up the scent of fresh tacos long before Shannon's. "Oh, now I know why you are pulling me this way."

Unfortunately there was no time for street dining, and the Squad had to dash by all the food. Out of nowhere, a piece of broiled chicken flew toward Waddlin and, like a professional baseball player, she caught the treat in mid-stride. Shannon called out, "Thank you!" and the taco cook gave her a thumb's-up. *Maybe I like the city after all*, she thought as they hurried along.

The Rescue Squad picked up the pace and headed down a sidewalk that hadn't been in Smart's instructions. Shannon was a little confused; she stopped and looked around. The crowds of people had thinned out. *Where did they go?* She also noticed that the stylish steel-and-glass buildings had given way to old brick and tin offices and shops. And something else was different. Spray-painted art and writing started to appear on walls and fences. Some of the drawings were really interesting, but there were a lot of words Shannon didn't recognize. Big cars that were low to the ground drove slowly by, music blaring so loudly it pulsated right through Shannon. Waddlin didn't like the sound of the thumping music, and started to growl. Shannon patted her on the back, letting her know everything was going to be okay.

Then someone asked, "What are you doing around here?"

Shannon turned to see a young girl with a big, easy smile and dreadlocks. She was riding a scooter. "My name is Lakoiya," said the girl, "and I live down the street. What's your name?"

"Hi, Lakoiya. My name is Shannon, and this is Waddlin."

"Wow, Shannon, is this your dog?"

"Yep, she's my best friend."

"I've always wanted a dog, but our house is really

small. They call this part of town 'the Hood', but to me it's just home. I know everyone around here." Lakoiya gave Waddlin a big hug, and she returned the hello with a big slobbery kiss. Lakoiya laughed out loud. "Where do you live?" she asked Shannon.

"Out in the country, with my mom and dad in a little silver trailer."

"It looks like you're going on a hike with that backpack on Waddlin. So why are you in this part of the city?"

Shannon thought, *Lakoiya is not going to believe that I'm trying to find my friend Betty, who is a big silver bowl.*

Just then the drone crew zoomed by overhead.

"Hey! Did you see that?!" Lakoiya said, watching the drone as it circled in the sky above. Smart was showing off, doing twists and turns in the air.

"Wow, I've never seen a spaceship!"

"That's not a spaceship, it's my friends. Smart is my smart phone, flying a drone with Left and Right—"

Lakoiya interrupted. "You have your own smart phone!?"

Shannon was caught. "Well, no, it's my mom and dad's phone. I kind of borrowed it today."

"Oh, you're in trouble if they find out."

"I know, but I need to explain what's going on."

After Shannon explained everything, Lakoiya said, "Wow, it's so fine that you have a plan to save your friend. Can I help find Betty too?"

"For sure, you know this place better than we do."

Shannon was amazed that Lakoiya didn't make fun of her story and believed her. She knew they were going to be friends forever.

Smart made another perfect landing on the sidewalk,

and said "Hi" to everyone. Lakoiya couldn't believe what she was seeing. Then Left and Right started signing. Lakoiya jumped back. "What's with the dancing hands?"

Shannon laughed out loud and introduced Left and Right to Lakoiya, explaining what signing was. She told Lakoiya that Left and Right were glad to meet her.

"Wow," Lakoiya said. "Shannon, can you please teach me how to sign?"

"Sure, give me your right hand." In no time, Shannon taught Lakoiya to sign "Hi."

Waddlin decided it was a good time to lie down on a sunny part of the sidewalk. Salt and Pepper weren't too happy when Waddlin rolled over on top of them.

"HEY! We're getting flattened like pancakes!"

Waddlin jumped up and started sniffing the air at the word "pancakes."

Shannon giggled. "Sorry, Waddlin, no pancakes just now. But when we find Betty, we will have a pancake party celebration."

Remembering Betty, Shannon knew she needed to focus on the rescue mission and get back on track. "Okay, everyone, listen up. We need to keep moving because we only have a few hours before my mom and dad return home. They'll panic if I'm not there doing my Saturday chores."

From Shannon's tone of voice, everyone knew she meant business.

As Smart began to give Shannon directions to the diner, Lakoiya interrupted, sounding excited. "Shannon, I know a faster way to get to the diner from here. Sorry, Smart, but I live here and your GPS does not."

"No problem, Lakoiya, I'm all ears. Wait! I don't have ears! That's just a saying—"

"Okay, okay!" Shannon said to stop Smart from explaining his GPS system. "Let's get going!"

Waddlin leaped to her feet and put her nose to the ground. Smart quickly lifted off with Left and Right holding on, and Lakoiya took the lead, heading down the sidewalk on her scooter.

# CHAPTER 16

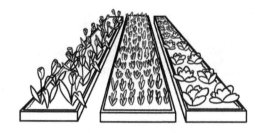

It was now a race to the diner to rescue Betty. Lakoiya, zooming ahead on her scooter, suddenly turned down a path through a vacant lot. "It's a shortcut!" she called over her shoulder to her new friends, who followed right behind. The path narrowed between old cars, forgotten furniture, and tall weeds. Shannon wasn't worried because she trusted Lakoiya to show the Rescue Squad the way.

To Shannon's surprise, they popped out onto a street lined with old trees, restaurants, a barbershop, and a donut shop. Weaving between shoppers, Shannon's nose was tickled by amazing aromas she'd never experienced before. *I bet Waddlin's nose is going crazy, she thought.*

As they passed a sidewalk café, a man sitting with a group of older neighbor friends called, "Hi, Lakoiya, why are you in such a hurry? Slow down! We don't want you to get hurt."

"Thanks, but we're in a hurry," Lakoiya replied as they hurried by. Little did these people know that Lakoiya was now part of a rescue squad looking for a lost silver bowl.

A few shoppers looked surprised to see this group

passing by with a drone overhead, while others never looked up at all and missed the whole scene. *Way too busy in their own little world, Shannon thought. Just like the people getting off and on the bus.*

She caught up with Lakoiya and asked, "Are we almost there?"

"Yep, one more turn."

As the Rescue Squad turned the corner and then crawled through a small hole in a broken-down fence, they entered one of the most beautiful gardens Shannon had ever seen.

Lakoiya proudly said, "This is our Community Urban Garden. People who live in this part of the city can grow food for free here."

Taking it all in, Shannon asked, "Does every big city has a community garden like this?"

"I don't know, but here, most people don't have yards, so this is where families grow fresh fruits and vegetables," Lakoiya said.

Shannon had never seen a lovelier garden. Not a single weed was in sight. She thought the natural tapestry of many colors next to old city buildings was beautiful, even though it was very different to the green countryside surrounding her own garden. *No way was I expecting a place like this when I stepped off the bus.*

Nearby, a woman was talking and laughing with an elderly man with white hair as they shared late-season goodies right out of the garden.

"Shannon, try one of these!" Lakoiya called, tossing a snap pea her way. Shannon opened up the pod and saw five green peas lined up perfectly. She grinned as she ate them. *These are better than my gummy bears.* Even

Waddlin got to enjoy a few snap peas, quickly gobbling them up.

"Hey, Lakoiya, put some in your pocket and we can eat them later," said Shannon. "We might need some energy. Let's go, we've got to find Betty!"

The Rescue Squad was on the move again.

# CHAPTER 17

As the squad quickly left the garden behind, Shannon asked again, "Lakoiya, are we getting closer to Bill's Diner?"

Lakoiya pointed across the street.

*No way!* Shannon thought, taking in the sad little diner across the street. Standing all by itself and rundown, it was like a forgotten orphan no one cared about. "It's almost lunch time and there isn't a soul in sight," she said.

"No one I know ever eats there," Lakoiya replied.

For a second Shannon wondered if Smart had gotten his Google search mixed up. Was Betty really stuck in this sad, rundown place so far from their wonderful home? *No matter what, we are going in!* Breaking in was out of the question, but sneaking in seemed like a good plan.

Between the rescue squad and the diner was a busy street with speeding cars flying by every second. Knowing it wouldn't be easy to cross, Shannon decided they'd be safer using the crosswalk. Looking both ways, the rescue squad started across the street, with Lakoiya in the lead. Shannon glanced up and saw a big delivery truck run a red light. Barreling down on them, it didn't look like it was going to stop. Shannon screamed "LAKOIYA!" and pulled her to safety just in time as the truck sped past and disappeared in traffic.

"That was way too close! What's wrong with that driver!" Lakoiya said in a low, terrified voice as she gratefully gave Shannon a hug for saving her life.

The Rescue Squad made it to the other side of the street and, still stunned, stopped to breathe. Shannon had her hand on Lakoiya's shoulder. "Are you okay?"

Lakoiya nodded. "But I'm still shaking. I just wish there was a witness."

Just then Smart landed the drone and announced, "I have it all on video, with the license plate and everything. I figured it would take you guys a few minutes to get across the street, so I lifted off for a quick test flight. I saw that truck heading right for you, Lakoiya, and tried to warn you, but I was too high up. Glad I'm good at videoing! I just sent my video clip to the police department."

"Good thinking, Smart!" Shannon said.

"Shannon, can you please hand me Smart for a second?" Lakoiya asked.

"Sure," she said, passing him over.

Lakoiya gave Smart a kiss on his little screen. Instantly a big red heart flashed on it. Everyone had a good laugh and then they headed for the diner to rescue Betty.

Two blocks over, in the donut shop the squad had passed earlier, Detectives Hardy and Mullins were enjoying a cup of coffee and a donut when Mullins's phone beeped. He checked it just as Hardy took a big bite of his chocolate-covered donut. "Mmmmm, best donuts in

73

town," he said. Then, noticing the frown on Mullins's face, he asked through a mouthful of chocolate, "Whatsup?"

"Well, this is interesting," said Mullins. "The chief just sent me this. Take a look." He held out his phone so that Hardy could watch Smart's video. Hardy's mouth dropped open, spilling rainbow sprinkles and bits of donut on the table. He mumbed something that sounded like "Wegofem!"

"If you just said, 'We got him,' then you're right," said Mullins. "We're going to run this speeder's license plates and then send it out to all units to make sure this guy's no longer behind the wheel."

Hardy nodded. "Who sent the video to the station?" he asked.

"Some guy named Smart," said Mullins.

"Smart? Are you sure?" asked Hardy.

"Yup, says so right here – Smart Peterson," said Mullins. "I'm going to call in that license plate, and then we'll send Mr. Smart a thank-you text."

"Right. Do we have time for another donut?" asked Hardy.

Mullins sighed and shook his head.

When the rescue squad was nearing the diner, Smart announced, "Wow, two detectives just replied! Listen: *Mr. Smart, thank you for the video and for being a concerned citizen. Thanks to the information you supplied, we have run the license plate on that truck, have identified the driver, and all units in the city are now looking for him. This reckless driver should be off the road soon, thanks to your help. Sincerely, Detectives Mullins and Hardy.*"

Lakoiya and Shannon high-fived, happy that the streets in the hood would soon be a lot safer.

As they reached the diner, Shannon gulped. *What's the plan?* She thought quickly. "You guys wait here," she said. "I'm going to see if the front door is open." Shannon had a feeling this Chef William guy and his diner were no longer in business. *So why would he take Betty from the park? He must just be a thief.*

The front door was as secure as a bank safe. Shannon sighed, feeling a heavy weight settle on her shoulders. She sadly announced the door was locked shut. All eyes were on her – the Rescue Squad could see she was in deep thought.

As she faced her friends, she noticed that a window on the side of the diner was slightly open. The gap was just wide enough for Left and Right to slip through.

"Guys – I have an idea," she said. "Left and Right, are you ready to find Betty?"

They stood at attention, saluted, and signed they were ready.

"You guys are the best!" Shannon said, and the whole Rescue Squad cheered. "Okay, guys, listen up – here's the plan. Left and Right, I'm going to put you through that open window. Your assignment is to scout out the inside of the kitchen, and then let us in through the back door. Got that?"

Without hesitation, Left and Right jumped into Shannon's open hands, and everyone wished them well.

"Now, Smart," Shannon said, "you are going to sit in that open window and use your flashlight app to help guide Left and Right around the kitchen."

"I'm ready," Smart said, but when he turned on the flashlight he noticed his battery charge was getting desperately low. *Not good*, he thought, but he made sure no one saw his concern.

"Okay, let's go," Shannon said. Left and Right held hands as Shannon put them through the window. Smart was shining the light on them, just like the spotlight on a circus act.

Just before jumping, Left signed to Right, "Remember we are Koa wood!"

"Yes!" Right signed back. And after a perfect landing in the dark kitchen, Left and Right took a playful bow and Smart laughed out loud.

Beyond Smart's dimming light, the kitchen was cold, dark, and creepy, like an abandoned house.

Smart whispered, "You guys better find a light switch quickly. My battery is at extremely low."

Left and Right signed, "Oh no."

A second later, the dark kitchen came to life. Left and Right had found the light switch. But they were shocked to see that the kitchen was as bare as a bone, without a plate, pan, or a big silver bowl in sight.

"What do you guys see?" called Shannon from outside. "Is Betty in there?"

For a long moment, not a word came back. Then a voice rang out in the deserted kitchen. "Hello, who's there?"

Left and Right froze, realizing they didn't have time to escape back out the window. It was a long drop to the counter, and there was no way to climb back up! Hearing footsteps getting closer, they signed to each other, *What do we do!?*

Outside, Shannon and Lakoiya had seen the kitchen light come on. Then they heard the voice ring out again. "Can I help you? Who's here?"

The girls looked at each other. Without saying a word

they knew what the other was thinking. The voice sounded kind and caring, and not at all angry that someone was possibly trespassing.

Suddenly an older gentleman appeared before Left and Right.

"Well, hello, little guys. Don't be afraid. My name is Curly."

Left and Right started to sign a shaky "Hello."

"Oh, you sign? Me, too," Curly said kindly. "My lovely wife was hearing impaired and signed all her life. So nice to meet you both."

At the same time, Shannon gave Lakoiya a leg up so she could see what was happening with Left and Right. Curly saw Lakoiya peeking through the window and signed, "Oh, you have a friend with you."

Left and Right signed back. "Yes, her name is Lakoiya, and she lives near here."

Curly turned and waved. "Hello, Lakoiya. Nice to meet you. My name is Curly."

"How do you know my name?" she asked, surprised.

Curly smiled. "Your two little friends told me, and I've seen you before at the urban garden. I'm friends with Daisy."

"Oh yeah, I've seen you there before. I see you met Left and Right?"

"Yes, we just met. Who's holding you up out there?"

"My friend Shannon."

"Well, be careful. Why don't you and Shannon come to the back door?"

"Yes, sir," Lakoiya said.

"Lakoiya, who is that?" Shannon asked.

"It's Curly, he knows my friend Daisy. He's really old and seems super nice."

"Are you sure we should go in?" Shannon asked, a little concerned.

"Yes," Lakoiya said. "Trust me – I don't think we have anything to worry about."

Curly picked up Left and Right in his gentle, big hands and carried them like baby chicks. Left and Right felt completely safe.

Salt and Pepper were still in Waddlin's backpack with the gummy bears, wondering what was going on. "Hey, what's happening?" they asked out loud.

As the Rescue Squad made their way to the back door, Shannon and Lakoiya both said, "We'll soon find out."

Everyone headed to the back entrance, with Waddlin in the lead pulling Shannon as if saying, "We're going to find Betty!"

The door cracked opened and there stood Curly, with Left and Right cupped in his hands. Curly's hair was almost white; he was a little hunched over, and rather wobbly on his feet. It was like meeting a loving great-grandpa.

"There you all are. Welcome, and please come in. Waddlin can come in, too."

"How do you know her name?" Shannon asked.

It didn't seem like Curly heard the question; he just eagerly waved everyone into the kitchen. As they all walked by him on their way in, Curly winked at Shannon, letting her know he'd known Waddlin's name all along.

The kitchen was empty. "Oh no," Shannon said in a low, sad voice, her heart sinking as she realized Betty wasn't there. *This can't be happening*, she thought, barely able to take another next step. Following behind, Lakoiya ran right into her.

"Don't worry, Shannon, we'll find Betty," Lakoiya said,

urging Shannon forward into the kitchen. But as Shannon looked around again there was still no Betty, and she felt as empty as the kitchen.

Curly asked everyone to gather around. "I'm so glad you all stopped by. We just closed a few days ago, and not much is happening around here. I've worked in this place as the bookkeeper for a long time, and it's never been so quiet."

Shannon felt sorry for Curly, and for a brief moment forgot all about Betty.

Curly was still carefully holding Left and Right in his hands as he turned to the group and said, "I'm sorry – your friend Betty is not here."

Shannon thought, *How does he know about Betty?*

Their echoing voices gave the kitchen an eerie, empty, almost haunted atmosphere. Curly gently tapped Shannon on the shoulder and in a caring voice said, "Have faith. I know you will find your good friend Betty."

"But how?" said Shannon, looking into the wise face of this old man who seemed to know her thoughts and the future. She believed Curly, but didn't really know why.

Lakoiya put her arm around Shannon.

Strengthened by Lakoiya's simple act of friendship and by Curly's understanding smile, Shannon knew they would eventually find Betty. But she also knew it wouldn't be today. And as much as she didn't want to leave, the time clock was ticking away in her mind.

"Curly, sir, it was very nice to meet you. But we need to catch a bus back home."

Curly smiled. "Yes, before your mom and dad return home from shopping."

*How in the world did he know that about my mom and dad?*

79

# CHAPTER 18

Sometimes getting everyone's attention was like herding chickens. Shannon knew the Rescue Squad were contemplating their next steps, but the thought of her mom and dad arriving home first wouldn't leave her mind.

"Where do we go now?" asked the squad.

To their surprise, Shannon sadly announced, "Home."

"What?!" said Salt and Pepper. "You're giving up too easily!"

Left and Right signed that they wanted to keep looking.

Waddlin looked sad, as if saying, *But we can't stop looking for Betty.*

Smart's battery was now so low he couldn't say anything – it wasn't often Smart was without comment.

Shannon asked Lakoiya if she could please guide them to the bus stop where Ms. Weasel dropped them off earlier that day.

As they waved goodbye to Curly, Lakoiya hopped on her scooter and said, "Okay, everyone, let's go. Follow me."

The pace was a little slower than earlier in the day,

when they'd been in a race against time to find Betty. Shannon still felt sad they hadn't found her, and also wondered how she was going to say goodbye to her new best friend, Lakoiya. They lived in two different worlds and miles apart, one in the country and one in the hood.

Between Lakoiya leading the way and Waddlin keeping her nose to the ground, Shannon expected the Rescue Squad would be arriving at the bus stop just in time. When they reached it, they saw a long line of people waiting. Most were reading the paper or staring at their phone. In Shannon's backpack, Smart was currently taking a long nap. *A lot of good Smart is now*, Shannon thought. *He's going to be so embarrassed when he recharges.*

Not a soul noticed the Rescue Squad. It was just another day in the big city for the robot-like people about to step aboard the bus. Shannon saw Lakoiya looking down at her feet, and knew it was time to say goodbye. Lakoiya handed Shannon Joe's drone, which Shannon almost forgot.

"Thanks for carrying the drone," she said. "I don't need a missing drone in my life too!" They laughed at the same time, which made saying goodbye a little easier.

"Lakoiya, it was so cool to meet up with you today. You helped me and the Rescue Squad so much. I know we would have gotten totally lost without you."

"No worries," Lakoiya said, beaming with a big smile. "I'm glad I helped you guys find the diner. I just wish Betty had been there – but we will find her."

Shannon sadly nodded. "Thanks, Lakioya, I know we will. I'll call you tomorrow, and don't worry, this time I'll ask my mom if I can borrow her phone."

Lakoiya laughed, and Shannon grinned.

"Bye, Lakoiya."

"Bye, Shannon."

Both girls were sad to say goodbye and made little eye contact. Lakoiya got down on one knee, gave Waddlin the biggest hug, and said, "I love you." Waddlin's butt was wagging as fast as her tail. Then Lakoiya took off on her scooter as quickly as possible.

Shannon watched as Lakoiya sped away. After she had disappeared from view, Shannon didn't move – not even when she heard the Rescue Squad saying they had to board the bus before it left without them. Shannon was sad she forgot to tell Lakoiya she was officially part of the Rescue Squad and a friend for life.

# CHAPTER 19

"Young lady, you've got to get on the bus. We are about to leave."

Shannon was so relieved not to hear Ms. Weasel's voice. She looked into the bus and saw a large man with a big white beard and long white hair behind the wheel. *If he was wearing red, he'd look just like Santa!* She took hold of Waddlin', held onto Joe's drone and in one step was on her way to leaving the big city.

"Sir, I only have five dollars and I need to get back home."

"Not a problem," the bus driver said. "Keep the money, you may need it. We will get you and your dog home safely. Welcome aboard." He reached into a jar near his seat and gave Waddlin a dog biscuit for the ride home. "We have lots of dogs that ride this bus, so I make sure they all get a treat. You have your hands full, young lady, with that deluxe drone. Don't worry, you can use a seat to store it."

*I wish Joe was here. That would've made his day.* "Thank you, sir," Shannon said as she and Waddlin walked past the driver and found a seat. She felt better when she had secured Joe's drone with a seat belt in the next row. *That's one less thing to worry about.*

The bus pulled away from the curb with Shannon's nose pressed to the window and Waddlin on the seat next to her. She replayed today's rescue attempt over and over in her mind.

*We really tried,* she thought. Shannon was happy the Rescue Squad was on the bus and safe. She was now realizing she risked their lives going to the big city. *I've learned a big lesson today.*

Her breath had misted the bus window, and she drew Betty with a happy face. It reminded her that Curly told her to have faith, and that he knew Shannon would find Betty and that she was safe for now.

As the bus picked up speed, the city's gigantic steel and glass buildings were soon left behind, and it seemed the whole day had faded away as rapidly as it started. Looking at her watch, Shannon saw that it was now approaching the time her parents would be heading home. Her mind started racing, for she was again fighting her silent enemy, the clock.

Shannon quickly began to organize everything in her mind. Inside Waddlin's backpack, everyone was accounted for, including the gummy bears. She thought about the drone, and wondered how she could repay Joe for loaning it to her. *Maybe another kiss? Ackk, what am I thinking?*

Smart was sound asleep because his battery was now completely dead. *I really miss Smart bossing everyone around, but I also just miss him.*

Shannon was hungry, and suddenly remembered the snap peas that were still in her pocket. One by one she enjoyed the little green natural treats that took her thoughts back to the most amazing garden in the middle of the hood.

As Shannon looked out the window, she saw lots of trees, green pastures and small family farms, which meant she was getting close to home. Soon, the bus slowed down and the noise from the brakes told her that the failed rescue mission was officially over.

The nice bus driver said, "I think this is your stop, young miss."

*So much different than Ms. Weasel!* Picking up the drone she waved goodbye to the driver, who gave Waddlin a loving pat on the head as they passed him.

Shannon was back on a country road she knew well. "Come on, Wadd, we're going home!" she said. There was no rush of humanity, just a rush of emotions knowing they were safe and almost home.

Shannon's pace quickened, and before long she was running home as fast as her legs would take her. The country air was fresh and sweet, and it was the fuel Shannon needed. Even though she'd been gone only half a day, it felt like much longer. Her adventure in the big city had felt rather unreal, while her home in the country was real. She knew why she was running as fast as she could up the road – it was towards the place she called home.

When Shannon reached the little silver trailer, she shouted, "We did it!" The note she'd left for Norma was still on the front door. She grabbed it and stuffed it in her pocket. She was home sweet home, had beat her parents back, and got rid of the evidence. *Phew!*

Once inside, Shannon thought *No time to rest. Mom and Dad will be home soon*. She took the backpack off Waddlin, who took a big stretch, yawned, and went to get a well-deserved drink of water from her dog bowl before scouring the kitchen floor. Shannon quickly plugged in Smart and was looking forward to her talkative little friend waking up from his sleep. Salt and Pepper, along with Left and Right, were back on the kitchen counter. It was good to see everyone back home, but Betty was still missing. It was hard for Shannon not to think they failed her, but again she reminded herself how Curly said she would find Betty.

But *how and when?!*

Shannon was so tired all she wanted to do was lie down on the couch and fall asleep. Then she saw the drone on the table. *Oh no, I've got to get this back to Joe!*

The next moment she was running out the door again and taking a shortcut through the garden, on her way to Joe's house. She ran as if it was an Olympic gold medal final, stopping only long enough to pick a bunch of fresh wild berries for Joe. In the blink of an eye, she was standing in front of him. "Joe, this is such a cool drone, thank you for trusting me with it."

"Shannon – I'm glad you like it. Did you get to fly it?"

"Sorry, Joe, I did not – but Smart did."

"Wow, you mean your mom's phone flew my drone?"

"Yep," was all Shannon could say. She could tell he was super happy to have his drone back, and she was super glad to have berries to give him instead of a kiss.

As Shannon arrived home, things were going to plan. Waddlin was sound asleep in her dog bed and Shannon heard not a sound from the Rescue Squad. She flopped on to the couch and thought about her amazing adventure. She couldn't wait to tell her mom about Lakoiya, and wanted to ask if she'd drive her back to the city to see her one day. Then she suddenly realized, *Uh oh, Mom has no clue about any of this! But I need to tell her the truth, even if I'll be in so much trouble.*

Shannon always told her mom everything, and felt ashamed she hadn't told her the truth earlier that day, even though she felt Mom would understand. Maybe? Hopefully? Then, like Waddlin, Shannon was soon sound asleep.

Shannon woke to the sound of the little Bug and gulped, for she knew she needed to tell her mom everything. A moment later she heard the sound of Waddlin's tail happily thumping against everything in its wake as she greeted Mom and Dad.

"Shannon, we're home," her mom announced as they opened the front door.

"Hi, Mom!"

"Hi, sweetie. Can you believe it? I left my mobile phone home today! Look, it's right where I left it." Both Mom's and Dad's hands were full of their reusable bags, which they put on the small dining room table.

Shannon didn't say a word, and felt bad inside.

"You're on the couch. You should be outside. It's beautiful out," said her dad as they started to unload the day's bounty.

*If you only knew!*

It was so good to hear her parents' voices, another confirmation that she was home sweet home and not in the big city.

"Did you get the chores done?" Mom asked.

"Yeah ... kinda," Shannon said quietly.

"That doesn't sound like you, Shannon. Are you okay?"

"Kinda."

"Okay, two kinda's in a row. What's up?"

Shannon took a deep breath. "We've got to talk, Mom, is that okay?"

"Sure, Shannon, how about over fresh brownies? I need a pick me up after running around with your dad all morning."

"Thanks, Mom, that would help."

"Well, speaking of help, why don't you help me make the brownies?"

Shannon was up in a split second and heading towards the kitchen, her mom on her heels. "Mom, have you ever tried brownies with crushed-up peppermint? They are so good!" Shannon was doing her best to keep her mom's focus on what they were about to mix and put in the oven. *Oh boy, this is going to be a big batch of headaches.*

As they made the brownies, not a word was said. The silence was so new and strange to Shannon. She could tell Mom knew something was up, and was waiting for Shannon to say what that was.

Finally she said, "Mom, I know where Betty is. I mean, I know she's lost. I know where she was, but she's not there any more. We couldn't find her."

"Wait," said Mom. "You just lost me. And Betty who?"

Shannon quickly realized she was getting stuck in her own, big, self-made web.

"What are you trying to tell me, Shannon?"

*Okay, here goes* ... "Mom, I went to the big city by myself today, after you and Dad left. I was trying to find Betty -- she's our bowl, remember?"

Mom didn't say a word. She just pulled up a small stool and sat down with her arms crossed.

"And in the city, I met a new friend; her name is Lakoiya.

Also, you didn't leave Smart – I mean your phone – here. I borrowed it. No, I stole it. Oh, I'm so sorry!"

Smart spoke up. "It's all my fault."

"What?!" Mom yelped. Was her phone talking without her giving it a command?

Then all of a sudden Salt and Pepper were walking on the counter towards her, telling her in broken English that it wasn't Shannon's fault.

Shannon could see her mom wondering if she was seeing things.

Left and Right were signing, looking like they were dancing in place – but they were trying to explain what happened. Shannon's fingers were a blur as she quickly replied.

When the story was told and everyone settled down, Holly, despite her shock, stood up and hugged Shannon. "These are your imaginary friends, aren't they?"

Shannon nodded, thinking, *Wow. This is going to be okay.*

But the "okay" didn't last long. Mom released Shannon and said, with disbelief, "Wait – the *city*? You went into the city by *yourself*?"

Shannon started backing up, looking for an escape route. The Rescue Squad had quickly disappeared, leaving Shannon and her mom in the tiny little kitchen. Even Waddlin had escaped to the garden, thinking it was a good time to hunt for snails. *Okay*, Shannon thought, *now it's all going in the wrong direction and it's all my fault.*

Then Mom smiled. "Shannon, I'm so glad you're home and safe, but you took a very big risk this morning, along with not being truthful. That can't happen again, do you understand? You know you can ask or tell me anything and I'll try my best to help you. Please give me a big hug and tell me you will never do that again."

"I won't, ever, I swear!" Shannon said, hugging her mom.

Out of nowhere the Rescue Squad reappeared and started cheering as Mom smiled. Shannon walked over to the dining room table, where family talks always took place, and told her mom the whole story.

Afterwards, Mom said, "Wow," and then with a smile told Shannon she was grounded for a month. Shannon understood and gave her mom a big hug.

After she and Mom had finished almost all the brownies, Shannon asked if Mom would drive her to the city, someday soon, to visit Lakoiya.

"That's a much better idea than your last plan!" said Mom.

They both laughed. Life was good at the moment, but Shannon was still thinking about Betty, her lost friend, and wondering where she was now and what had happened to her.

# CHAPTER 20

Betty felt like she had been held captive forever, even though it was just a few days. As time clicked by she missed her new family even more. Her kidnapper William was downright wicked to the bone, but Betty forgave him. The longer she was captive in the diner's kitchen, the more she could tell his cooking skills weren't the best, and that's why things weren't going so well at the diner. No one would ever dare say that to William, though, since they needed their jobs.

William had been known to wait out by the back door each night until his employees left the diner. Before he let them go, he would ask them to empty their pockets to make sure they weren't stealing from him. He just couldn't figure out why he was losing money. But if he waited at the front door of the diner, his customers would have told him. It was because the food he made was awful!

Betty loved tricking William. It was her way of having a little fun while held captive in the kitchen. When William was baking and adding ingredients to Betty, she waited for him to turn his back and then mischievously mixed everything up so he couldn't see what he had already added. He would come back, look into Betty, scratch his head, and yell at the top of his lungs, "I must be losing my mind!"

Betty would also spin away and hide or land in another part of the kitchen. William would scream, "Where is that mixing bowl with the dent? I was just mixing in it right here!" Betty always felt bad, but it was too much fun, and her way at getting back at William for taking her from her family.

*Oh, how I miss the farm,* Betty would often think, when she had to work with over-processed ingredients. Cooking at home on the farm was a joy for Betty, her friends and Shannon. When the crew was missing an ingredient, someone would simply go out the dog door and visit the hen house, garden, or orchard and get what they needed. It was as if the farm and neighborhood was a giant natural food pantry, because sharing food was as common as saying *good morning.*

One day, when Betty was placed on a rack after being washed clean, she noticed a cookbook sitting on a shelf. It was titled *Cooking Only Naturally.*

*What is a book like that doing in this place?* she thought. Then she noticed something handwritten on the cover. She flew over to the book for a closer look. "Chef Andre" it said. *Who is Chef Andre? He certainly doesn't work here.*

Every day Betty was sad to see all the uneaten food come back from the dining room and go straight into the trashcan. *What a waste,* she thought. William would always blame the cooks when the diners didn't finish their meals, but everyone knew they didn't because Chef

92

William didn't use good ingredients!

William had such a bad attitude and was such a terrible chef that it was obvious he was going to go out of business. Little did Betty know that this was Chef William's second attempt at owning a diner.

# CHAPTER 21

*How am I ever going to find Betty?* Shannon couldn't get this thought out of her mind. Now grounded, there was no way she could risk repeating another rescue attempt into the big city. And Betty could be anywhere.

At dinnertime Shannon wandered into the kitchen, wishing she would see Betty on the counter, smiling and ready to help with dinner. The empty counter told Shannon she might never see Betty again, ever. *Okay, then*, Shannon thought, *what would Betty do? Start cooking!*

Shannon looked at the refrigerator and thought, *This will be fun. I have no clue what's in there, but I just want to cook!* She heard the Rescue Squad stirring on the counter, lost and sad.

"Hi, guys. I know how you feel. Let's cook a fun dinner in honor of Betty. How about blueberry pancakes?"

"We can help," the Rescue Squad all said together.

Smart was way ahead of everyone. He loaded a bunch of blueberry pancake recipes on his screen.

Salt and Pepper voiced their concern about eating breakfast at night, but Shannon reassured them it was okay and that a lot of people enjoy a breakfast-style dinner once in a while. Then she asked her parents, "Hey, Mom and Dad, how do blueberry pancakes and scrambled eggs sound for dinner?"

"Delicious!" they both said.

The Rescue Squad became believers, and before everyone knew it, Left and Right had the blueberries washed and ready to make smiley faces on top of the pancakes!

With Smart supplying some fun music, everyone was working together and having a good time, but also thinking that one member of their band was sadly missing. Except Waddlin, who was thinking about a pancake "nibbie" hitting the floor. That would make her day!

After dinner, Shannon and her mom were busy doing the dishes while Dad read on the couch and the Rescue Squad went to bed. The girls were up to their elbows in dishes and suds. "Mom, I'm so sorry for not being honest with you, I really blew it. Please forgive me."

"Shannon, I forgave you the minute you told me."

"Why?" Shannon asked, a perplexed look on her face. "I was not honest, Mom."

"If I don't forgive you when you blow it, how would I ever expect to be forgiven when I blow it? And trust me, no one's perfect. So, Shannon, please forgive me." Then she soaked Shannon with a wave of dishwater.

For Shannon and her mom, washing dishes together was their special time to talk. However, today was filled with life lessons.

As they were drying off, Shannon knew the time was right. "Mom, I want you to meet Lakoiya."

"Who?"

"My new friend I met today, in the city," Shannon said.

"Oh, right. I remember you telling me about her."

"She is so cool, and I really want to be friends with her, but we are miles apart. And we don't even have our own cell phones."

"Now, Shannon, you know how I feel about cell phones before the age of thirteen."

*Guess I won't mention drivers' licenses then!*

"But I would love to meet your new friend," Mom continued. "Why don't you give Lakoiya a call and we'll try and visit next Saturday? How does that sound?"

Shannon gave her mom the biggest hug. "Thank you so much, Mom!"

"You're welcome, honey. I'm happy you met Lakoiya and I want to thank her for helping you through the city."

"Mom, Lakoiya calls were she lives 'the hood'."

"What?"

"Lakoiya says everyone calls it 'the hood' but to her it's just home."

Mom thought for a moment and then said, "I really do want to meet this young lady. She sounds very special."

It was Monday morning, and for the first time in a while Shannon was actually excited about heading back to school. It would give her an opportunity to slide back into her normal routine, racing Joe to the bus stop, seeing all her friends, and setting aside the big city adventure for a while. She had a big geography test at school and was totally ready. This was her favorite subject now, and in a way her adventure in the city gave Shannon a taste of discovery.

Back home, Holly was enjoying some quiet time curled up on the couch, alone with a book. It wasn't often Holly had the farm to herself, so she took full advantage of the occasion. Thanks to her book, she was now on the island of Maui in the late-1800s, surfing, along with others in the small village. Every so often, she would glance up from the beach and look out the window at the blazing colors of fall. Holly thought how wonderful it was that reading allowed you to be in two worlds at the same time.

A little while later, Holly heard a car drive up and figured David was home. She slipped back into the book, waiting for the sound of the door opening. Instead, she heard a loud KNOCK, KNOCK at the front door.

"Who could that be?" she wondered out loud. It was probably Norma, their neighbor down the street with the Jersey cows, dropping off some fresh cheese. As Holly made her way to the door, she was already dreaming about fun recipes to make with cheese. She opened the door, saying, "Hi, Norma–" but stopped when she saw two detectives flashing their badges.

"Good morning, Ma'am. I'm Detective Mullins and this is Detective Hardy."

Instantly Holly thought of Shannon and David, and hoped they were safe.

The short detective said, "We would like to talk to Smart Peterson. Is he available?"

Holly laughed and said, "Yep, let me see if Mr. Smart is available. Can you please wait?"

"Yes, Ma'am," the officers said at the same time.

As Holly turned to retrieve Smart, she wondered why in the world the police wanted to talk to her mobile phone.

"Smart," Holly called out, "two nice detectives would like to talk with you!"

97

Smart was right where she left him, on the small table by the couch.

"I was expecting them," Smart responded.

"What?" Holly said with a puzzled look as she picked him up.

"Yes, I emailed the police department a video of the truck that almost ran Lakoiya over when we were searching for Betty in the city," he explained, as Holly carried him to the front door.

*You little rascal*, Holly thought, rolling her eyes. "Officers–"

"Detectives, Ma'am."

"Oh, that's right, I'm so sorry." Holly handed Smart to Detective Hardy. "This is Smart Peterson."

"Hello, Detectives, I'm glad you stopped by and I'm happy to answer any questions."

The detectives had no clue how to question a witness that was a smart phone. Detective Hardy, acting like he was holding a hot potato, tried to pass Smart to Detective Mullins.

He refused to take it and said, "Er, Mr. Smart, thank you for sending us the video. We have apprehended the suspect and suspended his license to drive."

Detective Hardy said, "We could use someone like you down at the police station."

Smart couldn't believe what he'd just heard, and flashed a detective badge and smiley face on his screen.

Smart couldn't wait to tell Lakoiya and Shannon that the reckless driver would soon no longer be terrorizing the city. Smart also was going to brag a little that one of the detectives mentioned he could join the police force.

The detectives thanked Smart and Holly for their time.

They tipped their hats, and Detective Hardy handed the witness back to Holly with a smile.

Heading back to their car, Hardy said, "Well, that call went down in my history book."

"Yeah," Mullins agreed, "I can't remember ever interviewing a smart phone as a witness."

"That's for sure," Hardy added.

# CHAPTER 22

Saturday finally came, and the morning sun shone bright through Shannon's little trailer window. Waddlin was asleep at the end of the bed.

Shannon woke to the aroma of brewing coffee wafting its way through the trailer and knew breakfast wasn't far away.

Thoughts of last weekend's adventure were still rolling around in her memory. She couldn't wait to relive her big city adventure with her mom in tow.

"Shannon, are you awake?" Mom yelled from the kitchen.

"I'm awake, Mom."

Waddlin was now in midair, and with a few strides would be in her favorite place in the trailer – the kitchen. Another fun morning had begun.

After breakfast, the sound of the little red Bug warming up in the driveway sent Shannon to a whole new level of excitement. Soon she would be heading back to the city to meet up with Lakoiya and, more importantly, continue the search for Betty. As Shannon was heading out the door, she paused for a second, turned and ran back into the trailer -- she needed the Rescue Squad. She grabbed Left and Right off the kitchen counter, and Salt and Pepper, who were in the middle of their beauty sleep. Shannon was learning to listen to the quite voice inside herself.

Mom was patiently waiting. Shannon quickly grabbed Smart off the counter.

"Mom forgot you again! You're coming with us!" she said, and raced to the car.

Waddlin was already in the back seat with her head out the window, as if to say, "Hurry up, Shannon, I'm ready to go!"

Shannon handed Smart to her mom. "Oh thanks," she said. "I almost forgot my phone, just like the other day." Mom and daughter both chuckled and with that, off they went to the big city.

Thinking about her first secret mission, Shannon had mixed feelings, but today's trip felt much better since she had planned it with her mom rather than secretly behind her back. Shannon gave thanks for having such a wonderful friend who just happened to be her mom.

As they drove off, Shannon could see Waddlin in the side mirror. Her head was out the window, ears sticking straight up, and the biggest wind smile ever on her face.

As Mom drove towards the city, the change from country to urban to hood was underway again. It was like spring to summer to fall. The little red Bug made its way into the city between the semi-trucks and buses, like a tiny ladybug moving through a big garden. This time the city didn't feel as scary either. Perhaps that was because Shannon was with her mom. The sounds of fast-moving cars and people were no longer strange. Shannon realized there was a rhythm to it all, as there was a rhythm to the country, but the city moved at a much faster tempo.

Suddenly Smart shouted, "Turn left on Senate Street in five-hundred feet."

Shannon laughed to herself as she remembered Smart directing the Rescue Squad through the city last time. It was good to have him in command again, and she knew it made Smart happy.

As Shannon was reminiscing, her mom said, "I'm getting hungry, how about you?"

"Yeah, me too, Mom. Turn right at the next light and just a block up there are some amazing food trucks."

"Shannon, how did you know that?" They looked at each other, and Shannon saw Mom remembering her little girl was just here last week without her.

As they approached the food trucks, Holly got lucky and found a parking spot with time still on the meter. Her and Shannon's stomachs were growling and Waddlin's nose was in overtime. Everyone in the car was now starving and thought only about fresh veggie tacos with extra guacamole. The aroma of food from all over the world was thick in the air – Chinese, Mexican, African, and Greek.

Shannon and her mom could barely keep up with Wadd, and Shannon was amazed her four-legged friend remembered the taco truck from the rescue attempt.

"The three hundred million olfactory receptors in Waddlin's nose are guiding her to the taco dude. We only have six million in our noses," Shannon said.

"How in the world did you ...? Oh never mind," Holly said, surprised and impressed at her daughter.

Shannon looked at her mom and grinned.

They stopped in front of a truck. "Hey, I know you guys," said the man serving. "My name is Carlos. What would you like to try today?"

"I remember you too," said Shannon. "How about some veggie tacos?"

Carlos said proudly, "We have the *best!*"

After eating every last morsel, all agreed Carlos's tacos *were* the best! Even Waddlin was treated to her very own K-9 taco, compliments of Carlos, who said he'd had a dog named Lucky when he was a kid, it had looked just like Waddlin, and was his best friend ever.

Between the tacos and the freshly made horchatta, Mom thought they would need naps, but Shannon was again fighting the clock in her head. "Mom, we have to go, but I can't wait to bring Dad back someday soon for some of Carlos's tacos!"

As they walked away from the food trucks Shannon said, "I am so stuffed!" and stuck out her tummy like she did at the farmers' market. Mom laughed out loud and stuck hers out too. Shannon thought, *I love it when Mom acts like a kid!*

They all jumped back in the red Bug and quickly joined the swarm of cars heading through the center of the city. Captain Smart started barking out commands again: "Turn left in eight-hundred feet."

*Boy, I love my job*, Smart thought.

Before long the little red Bug pulled up at a stop sign. Sensing the moment was right, Smart asked, "Hey, Mrs. P., why don't you let me drive?"

"*What?*" Holly said in disbelief.

Shannon was also surprised, but figured Smart could easily drive the Bug. Her mom pulled over to the curb

103

and rested her head on the steering wheel. "*This can't be happening!*" she muttered.

"Don't worry, I have been researching self-driving car technology," Smart said proudly. "It's a free app."

Nobody said a word for a minute, then Holly announced, "Okay, let's go for it. Let's give Smart the wheel."

Shannon was in total shock. Did she hear that right?

"No way, thanks Mom!" she called from the back seat.

"Mrs. P., thank you for the vote of confidence!" Smart said.

"Okay, what do we do?" asked Holly.

"Just hold me up, Mrs. P.," said Smart, "so I can see out the window."

She did as he said, and off they went with all the windows down and the air of adventure whirling through the little red Bug.

They pulled up next to a car at the intersection. The other driver looked over and saw no one in the Bug's driver's seat. Mom returned his shocked look with a giant grin, and then waved as they drove away.

The driving experiment was going well until they heard a siren and saw the flashing lights behind them.

"Oh no, I'm in really big trouble now," Holly muttered.

"Mom, I'm so sorry," Shannon said in a worried voice.

A few seconds later, the police car went speeding by. Smart, like all the other drivers, had safely pulled over to the side of the road, as the law required. *Wow! That was a close call*, thought Shannon.

Once they realized they weren't going to jail, it became a quest to get to Lakoiya's house as quickly as possible, with the new test pilot driving the car.

Just like on her first trip to the big city, Shannon could tell they were leaving the downtown area and entering the hood, but didn't dare say a word. She could tell by her mom's body language that she had noticed the change as well.

"Shannon, are you sure we're going the right way?" she asked, concern on her face.

"Yep!" said Shannon confidently. "Don't worry, Mom. Smart knows where he's going."

Noticing the change in her tone, Smart chirped, "You've got nothing to worry about, Mrs. P.!"

"Uh, okay then,," was all Holly could say.

Shannon felt safer in the hood than in other parts of the city. Everyone Shannon had met on the rescue mission was super nice. The hood just had a bad rap – not the style of music that you hear throughout the hood but the impression people had of Lakoiya's home turf. *If only everyone knew how cool it really is here*, Shannon thought.

Then Smart announced, "We are getting close to Lakoiya's home." He made a sharp turn at the next corner, and there, before them, was a cute little brick house. Smart pulled the Bug into the driveway as Shannon happily announced, "We made it!"

Shannon could sense her mom breathing out in relief. And when she saw Lakoiya's scooter leaning on the steps, Shannon knew they'd found the right house. Seconds later Lakoiya was flying out the front door, her feet barely touching the steps.

"You're here! No way, dudette!"

Shannon and Waddlin jumped out of the car and a big three-way hug followed. This was so much better than the last hug, when Shannon and Lakoiya had to say goodbye after the failed rescue mission.

Shannon cheerfully introduced Lakoiya to her mom, who made sure Lakoiya knew how much she appreciated her helping Shannon. "It was a miracle you two crossed paths – thank you for helping Shannon on her first trip to the city."

"No worries, Mrs. Peterson. It was lucky for me we ran into each other, too. I now have a new best friend. I'm so happy to see the Rescue Squad again so soon."

Shannon started to laugh because Left and Right were trying to sign to Lakoiya from the backpack, and she could hear Salt and Pepper's muffled "hello."

Waddlin's whole body was wagging, which was her way of saying hello. Lakoiya gave her a bear hug, which Wadd repaid with a big, sloppy kiss.

Smart said, "Lakoiya, what's up?"

"Oh, hi, Smart. I see you drove everyone over today. I'll need to take some driving lessons in a few years – Shannon, too."

Holly shook her head in disbelief, but said, with a twinkle in her eye, "Smart, you did a fine job driving us today."

Lakoiya's mom came out of the house, smiling. "Welcome, everyone! My name is Shirley. Lakoiya's been so excited, waiting for you. Please come in and share the fresh Meyer lemon bars we just made."

As they made their way into the house, Shannon caught Lakoiya by the sleeve. "Can we show my mom that beautiful community garden around the corner later?"

"For sure. I know everyone at the garden and I know they'd love to share their harvest with us!"

Shirley's home was modern and simple, and art was displayed everywhere, like a tiny art gallery. Every room in the house was alive with brightly-colored paintings that revealed the beauty of the inner city.

Shannon and her mom wandered through the house as if they were taking a tour of an art museum, as Shirley and Lakoiya shared stories of each painting. The ideas the country girl and her mother had had about the hood were brushed away as they began to see the area through the strokes of Shirley's paintbrush.

Shirley finally announced, "Lemon bars wait for us!" As soon as everyone arrived in the kitchen, it felt like home to Shannon and Holly, as if they could start cooking right away, and would know where everything was.

Waddlin made a complete search of the kitchen but found no food to rescue or clean up. But she did find a nice sunny spot in which to lie down and enjoy a snooze. Life was good.

"Best lemon bars ever!" Holly proclaimed.

"Thank you. They were made with local Meyer lemons," Shirley said proudly.

"Local?" Holly asked.

"Why, yes. We don't have big farms or orchards in the city, but there are backyard fruit trees that sadly weren't being picked. Now a local nonprofit group's volunteers collect the unwanted fruit and deliver it to our community garden so everyone can share, and the fruit doesn't go to waste."

"About forty percent of our food in America does not make it to a kitchen table," Smart informed them.

"That's crazy," Shannon said. "So I would toss almost half my breakfast, lunch and dinner away each day. No way – how stupid is that!"

Shirley seemed to be surprised that a cell phone had spoken.

"Don't worry, Smart talks all the time," said Shannon, "and he just drove our car perfectly to your house."

"Say what?" Shirley said in shock. "You have to be kidding!"

"No joke," Holly said with a little laugh.

Smart's screen lit up with a thumb's-up emoji. "Thank you, Mrs. P.," he commented, with his volume on high.

Everyone laughed and enjoyed the homemade lemon treats. Soon not even a crumb was left on the platter.

Shirley said to Lakoiya, "Why don't you and Shannon ride the scooters to the community garden and we'll catch up with you."

"Okay, Mom, we'll see you over there."

The girls were out the door and heading down the sidewalk with Waddlin in tow and the crew in her doggie backpack.

As they cleaned up, Holly mentioned to Shirley that she noticed a photo of a solider, a framed medal, and folded American flag on the bookcase in the living room.

"Yes, that's Lakoiya's father. He was killed in action in Afghanistan."

"I'm so sorry," Holly said, and gave Shirley a hug.

"Thank you, Holly. We miss him every day. He was our hero. Lakoiya never really knew her father because she was just learning to walk when Don was deployed overseas. But she's grown up to be just like her dad – nonstop energy and very athletic. I see so much of Don in her. Lakoiya has had a hard time making friends at school and I'm so glad she met Shannon."

"I am, too," Holly said, holding Shirley's hand.

"How about we head down to the garden? I'll bring my basket and we can pick veggies for tonight's dinner, and you can take home whatever you want."

"I love that idea, fresh veggies from the hood," Holly said.

As the two new friends headed to the garden, Shirley said, "I've just got to ask, did your cell phone really drive your car today?"

"Yep," Holly said, grinning as Shirley shook her head with wonder.

It was a short walk to the community urban garden, and Holly was amazed at how big it was and how much it looked like a gigantic quilt of natural colors. She and Shirley spotted Shannon and Lakoiya being treated to some inner-city veggies grown by an elderly farmer. Shirley explained that Lakoiya was good friends with the woman, and helped almost every day in her tiny farm plot.

"Hi, Daisy," said Shirley. "This is my new friend Holly, whose daughter, Shannon, is enjoying your awesome garden goodies."

Daisy said hello, then explained that many people in the inner city depended on this community garden for most of their fresh vegetables. "This special garden has nourished not only me, but has given me a wonderful way to love my neighbors. Without this garden, we wouldn't have many vegetables in our part of town."

All of a sudden, Smart's muffled voice came from the doggie backpack. "It's called a 'food desert', where only highly processed 'snack foods' are available and good healthy fruits and vegetables are very limited."

"But not anymore!" Daisy said with a proud smile.

"Thank you, Smart," Shannon said.

"No worries."

As they all strolled through the garden, the urban farmers made sure the girls sampled the season's best from their little plots. Shannon and Holly could see how proud the farmers were of their tiny farms. There were vegetables Shannon had never seen before, even at her local farmers' market.

Shirley said, "Just think of the community garden as a two-acre salad bowl."

"Wow, I never thought of it that way," said Shannon. She also made a mental note to ask Daisy if she'd come to her school and share her knowledge and experiences in urban farming when her school's garden was underway. Daisy would be a perfect mentor and everyone would love her.

After a while Lakoiya asked her mom, "Can I take Shannon over to the skate park? It's not that far away. I want to show her some tricks on my scooter."

"Sure, Lakoiya. We'll meet you over there with Waddlin."

"Cool – thanks, Mom," replied Lakoiya. She and Shannon picked up their scooters, put on their helmets, and raced away.

Lakoiya was in the lead and Shannon was right behind her. As they turned the corner, they found the sidewalk crowded with people window shopping, walking hand in hand, and enjoying the hood's main street. Lakoiya and Shannon didn't slow down, working the crowd like a ski slalom course.

"Hi, Lakoiya!" many of her neighborhood friends shouted out, as the two girls flew by.

Things got interesting when the street turned into a downhill run. Gravity worked its magic and the girls no longer had to push their scooters. Shannon had never gone so fast, and felt like she was flying.

All of a sudden, Lakoiya skidded to a stop. Shannon almost ran her over but just managed to avoid a big wreck. Laughing and catching her breath, she asked, "Why did you do that?"

Lakoiya smiled and pointed to a tiny shop. "Because this is the best donut shop in the world!"

"I don't know," Shannon said. "My mom doesn't want me to eat too much sugar."

"I think she won't care, especially if we bring donuts back for her and my mom, too."

"I love that idea, and I love maple bars," Shannon whispered to Lakoiya.

"Me, too," Lakoiya said with big grin.

As the girls rushed into the little shop, Shannon exclaimed, "Wow, this is no ordinary donut shop. The menu board says the donuts are made with all organic and natural ingredients. Even the milk is organic."

With their bagged donuts in their hands, the girls sprinted out of the shop, jumped on their scooters, and raced off towards the skate park.

After eating their donuts and – *oops!* – their moms' too, Lakoiya showed Shannon her tricks, stealing the spotlight at the park with her skills.

Finally, Holly and Shirley arrived. After watching their girls skate, clapping and hooting for them, the two moms headed over to the coffee truck for a little pick-me-up.

"Mom, we are going to skate a little longer," Shannon said.

"Yeah, I'm going to show Shannon a few new tricks," Lakoiya said with a big grin and high-five with Shannon.

"Okay, have fun and we will see you back at the house soon," the moms said as they headed back with Waddlin in tow.

# CHAPTER 23

The girls had just finished their session in the skate park when Shannon called out, "Lakoiya, did you see the van that just drove by?"

"What van?" Lakoiya asked, looking startled.

"The white one! I'm sure the chef who kidnapped Betty was driving!"

"How would you know that?"

"Because I saw the tattoo on his arm!" Shannon rode her scooter to get a better look down the street. "It was him, I'm a hundred percent sure!" She was now almost in the middle of the street, watching where the van was headed.

Lakoiya dropped her scooter on the sidewalk and ran to pull Shannon out of the street. "Shannon, come on, before you're run over!"

By the time they made it back to the sidewalk, Shannon was already heading in the same direction as the van on her scooter. "Shannon, wait up!" Lakoiya shouted. She wasn't used to being left in the dust on her scooter.

"Oh darn! The van's gone!" Shannon said as Lakoiya caught up with her.

"Which way did it go?"

"It turned right at that intersection," Shannon said, pointing.

"Then follow me," Lakoiya said excitedly. "It's a one-way street that curves back, and I know a shortcut."

The light turned green; they both checked traffic, and then flew through the crosswalk to the other side of the street. Lakoiya's shortcut took them through the graveyard where her grandma was buried. "Hi, Grandma!" Lakoiya yelled.

The narrow old road through the graveyard began to slope down towards the street below, and soon the girls felt like two Olympians in a downhill race. Lakoiya was in the lead but in a flash Shannon flew by. "Girl, you're flying!" Lakoiya laughed.

When they skidded to a stop at the bottom of the hill, Shannon pointed. "There it is!" In seconds, the van zoomed past.

"Shannon, I think it's headed back to the diner. And I saw the guy's tattoo, too. It's freaky!" Lakoiya yelled over the sound of the traffic.

At this time of day, the empty sidewalks were a private speedway for the scooters, and soon both girls zoomed up to the diner where the van was parked in the diners' lot.

"You were right, Shannon, that must be the mean dude who kidnapped Betty."

Shannon tapped Lakoiya's shoulder. "Yeah, look – the van's side door is open! Shhh, let's sneak up and see what's inside."

"Okay," Lakoiya whispered, "but be ready to blast out of here if things get weird."

Shannon nodded and led the way. Their heartbeats and footsteps seemed crazy loud.

As they carefully peeked around the open side door they were shocked!

"What a mess!" Shannon said, making a face and holding her nose. "There's no way Betty is in there."

"Shannon, is that you?" Betty's voice suddenly called out.

"Betty? No way!" Shannon said.

"You sure it's Betty?" asked Lakoiya.

"Yeah, it's me, it's me, Betty!"

"Oh my gosh, I can't believe we found you, Betty," said Shannon. "My friend Lakoiya's with me. Are you okay?"

Before Betty could reply, a loud and angry voice rang out from behind the girls. "What are you kids doing by my truck? Are you stealing stuff?"

"Yikes!" Shannon and Lakoiya yelped, and quickly backed up looking for a way out. They didn't want to leave Betty, but when they saw the mean man with the tattoo marching toward them, they grabbed their scooters and fled, escaping seconds before he reached the van and slammed the door shut. "Nosey kids!" he growled.

Inside the van, Betty's world was pitch black again. Unable to move, her hope vanishing, Betty began to cry for the first time. *That was Shannon! And that wicked Chef William frightened her and her friend off.*

The darkness felt as terrible as it had when she was stuffed in the box at the factory. *Not again, please!*

A ways up the street, Shannon and Lakoiya finally stopped and looked back at the van. They could no longer see the man with the tattoo.

"He's gone; what a loser!" Lakoiya said.

"I can't believe it, Lakoiya. Betty was just a few feet away from us. We've got to remember his license plate!" Shannon said.

"It said *Octopus*."

"Yeah," said Shannon. "Like the octopus tattoo swinging knives from each of its eight arms. He kidnapped my friend Betty, and now I know who he is and where he's holding her."

"Let's get back to my house and call the police," Lakoiya said.

"I have a better idea. Let's ask Smart if he can call his detective friends to help us find that van and Betty!"

"Okay, follow me!" Lakoiya said, and she zoomed off.

"You know *another* shortcut?" Shannon called, barely keeping up with her.

"Are you kidding?" Lakoiya yelled, and before long they were in the driveway, dropping their scooters, and running up the front steps of Lakoiya's house.

"Mom!" the girls both called as they ran through front door.

Holly and Shirley rushed out of the kitchen, the worried looks on their faces turning to relief when they saw their daughters.

"Where did you two go?" they asked together.

"You just took off and didn't tell us where you were going!" said Holly.

"We were worried and couldn't call you!" said Shirley.

"Well, if we had phones you could've called us," the girls said.

"You're right, but you are not thirteen yet ..." Holly told Shannon.

"... and you need to tell us your plans," finished Shirley.

Shannon said, "We know, but guess what happened!" And then the girls told their moms the whole story.

# CHAPTER 24

"No way," both moms said when the girls finished telling their story.

"How can we help?" Shirley asked.

"We need Smart to contact his two detective friends," said Shannon.

Smart dialed a number and switched on his speaker, while flashing a detective badge on his screen.

"Detective Mullins here," came a voice.

"Detective Mullins, this is Smart Peterson."

"Who?"

"I'm the smart phone you met."

They heard Mullins's muffled voice telling Hardy, "Remember the smart phone witness? It's him again."

Clearing his throat, Detective Mullins said, "Yes, Smart, good to hear from you. What can I do for you?"

"We need your help."

"We?" said Detective Mullins.

"Yes, my friends Shannon and Lakoiya, who was the girl in the video I sent you, found their friend Betty in a van. She's been kidnapped by a mean chef who owns the van."

"Smart," Mullins said, "this is very serious. Can you give me a description of Betty?"

"Yes, sir. Well, she is ... nineteen inches in diameter, and silver."

There was a pause. "Thank you, Smart, for the information, but we are a bit confused," Mullins said.

"Oh, well maybe this will help you," Smart said. "Betty is a bowl."

There was more silence on the other end. Then Mullins said, "A bowl? As in, a mixing bowl?"

"Yes, sir," Smart said. "That was great detective work."

"Uh, er, well, thank you, Smart. How about we stop by the farm?" said Mullins.

"But, detective, I'm not at the farm. I'm in the hood downtown."

"Oh. Then give us the location and we'll be right there!" said Mullins.

"No worries, Detective Mullins. I just sent you a text," Smart said.

"You're fast, Smart. I just got it, thanks, and we are on our way."

"Thank you, sir," Smart replied.

As the two detectives drove up to Lakoiya's house, Holly whispered to Shirley, "I've met these detectives before, and Hardy is maybe someone you should get to know, if you know what I mean." Holly winked and Shirley blushed.

Smart was the first to greet the detectives. "Thank you, detectives, for offering to help us find our friend Betty."

Mullins said, "Smart, we normally don't go looking for, uh, silver bowls, but for you we're willing to bend the rules."

Shannon stepped forward. "Sir, we can help. We know where the van may be."

Lakoiya nodded, saying, "Yeah, and I can take you there!"

"That's a bit unusual, but if your mothers agree ..." Mullins looked at Holly and Shirley, who both nodded. "Okay, girls, jump in and let's find that silver bowl."

Soon Shannon and Lakoiya were in the back of the unmarked police car, waving at their moms through the back window as they set off looking for Betty.

"Turn left in eight-hundred feet," said Smart.

Detective Hardy asked about the license plate.

"*Octopus*," Lakoiya replied. Shannon told the detectives that the kidnapper had a large octopus tattoo on his left arm, and that he was the chef who ran Bill's Diner.

"That place had the worst food in town, which is why it closed," Hardy said to Mullins, who nodded. "Remember when Chef Andre ran it?"

"Yes," said Mullins, "and I sure wish Andre was still the chef. He had the best food in town."

"Hardy!" Mullins shouted, so loud that Hardy jumped. "I just thought of something! Remember when we were called to investigate an irate customer at the thrift store a few days ago? The customer's left arm was covered with a big octopus tattoo!"

"Oh," said Shannon, "let's go there."

Smart spoke up. "I can save you three minutes' driving time. Turn right at the next intersection."

They arrived at the Back Door Thrift Store, and the detectives asked the girls to please wait in the police car. As they walked to the door, Detective Hardy said, "You ask about the silver bowl named Betty."

Mullins said, "*You ask*. And don't forget our ranks at

the department and that I'm your boss."

"All right," Hardy grumbled, "but you're buying donuts tomorrow."

When they entered the store, the two pulled out their badges and flashed them at the woman behind the counter.

"Hello, ma'am. I'm Detective Hardy and this is Detective Mullins. We would like to ask you a few questions."

The lady smiled. "Of course. And I see you boys all the time at the donut shop. Great place, isn't it? Why, I saw you there earlier. I love the chocolate-covered donuts with rainbow sprinkles too!" She winked and smiled.

"Er, yes," said Hardy, worried that anyone else in the store might be hearing this. After all, they were here on official police business, not to talk about donuts.

"How can I help you, officers?" she asked.

"Detectives, ma'am."

"Oh yes, I should have known. We get detectives in here looking for stolen goods all the time."

"Well, we too are looking for something." When Hardy didn't continue right away, Mullins nudged him. "A ... silver bowl."

"Oh, you like to cook!" said the woman.

"Er, no, ma'am. The bowl in question was kidnapped – er, stolen – and we're looking for the man who perpetrated the crime. His left forearm is covered with an octopus tattoo."

The woman became quite excited. "Yes! A man with that tattoo was just in here about an hour ago, with a box of things. When I said sorry, the store is stuffed and I can't take what you have, he became quite angry and rude. Why, he stormed out of here and said he would take this old kitchen junk to the recycle center. You know the place with the mountain of chewed-up metal? You can't miss that big mess. And after he left, I called to report him, just because he was so very nasty."

"Thank you, ma'am," said Mullins, "that's very helpful. We will check it out. Come on, Hardy."

They raced to their car and told the girls they just missed the chef and it looked like he was headed to the junkyard!

"OH NO!" Shannon and Lakoiya cried.

Smart turned up his volume and announced, "I just mapped the location, let's go!"

The car sped out of the lot with the siren on and lights flashing. The Rescue Squad was on the chase again!

# CHAPTER 25

Meanwhile, in the dark old van, Betty was starting to lose hope. But seeing Shannon even for a moment gave her faith this nightmare would soon come to an end.

The doors of the van suddenly opened. Betty hoped to see Shannon and Lakoiya, but instead there were two men who brought back memories of the workers at the factory where she was born. Betty instantly had a bad feeling. And then she heard that awful sound she never wanted to hear again. The metal shredder. It shook the ground, along with all of Betty's hopes of reuniting with her family.

The workers pulled Betty and the other pans out of the box and tossed them in a big metal bin. Betty did her best to escape but was knocked down by flying pots and pans falling on top of her. Dazed, Betty was again being held captive against her will. Every second, more weight pressed down on her, like a waffle iron. "Shannon, help!" she cried out. But no one replied.

The detectives' car screeched to a halt as it nearly crashed into a railroad crossing. When everyone straightened up and looked ahead, they saw a freight train moving slowly just in front of them. A few feet further and everyone would have been as flat as a pancake, crushed under the wheels.

"Is everyone okay?" Mullins asked as Harding exhaled loudly.

"YES!" Shannon, Lakoiya,  and Lakoiya -- and Smart -- answered.

Mullins put his head on the steering wheel and started breathing again.

The freight train was moving as slow as a tortoise, and then it came to a stop altogether. Shannon and Lakoiya looked at each other.

"This can't be happening!" said Shannon.

Their first instinct was to jump out and run across the tracks, but that would be way too dangerous.

"Smart, we need your help," announced Mullins. "Get us to the recycle center!"

"Yes, sir!" Smart replied.

Mullins put the police car in reverse; its wheels spun and the smell of burning rubber filled the air as the car did a complete 360-degree donut circle, and then another half-circle before heading off in the opposite direction.

"Wow … I'm impressed," Hardy said with a big grin.

Shannon couldn't believe what was happening. "This is more fun than the rides at the county fair!" she said wide-eyed to Lakoiya, as the world circled around them.

"Detective Mullins …" Smart called out, "take the next left, go two blocks, turn left one more time and we are there!" Then Smart started to ring.

"Oh no, it must be one of our moms," said Shannon. "Smart, can you please answer yourself?"

"Of course. Hello, this is Smart Peterson."

"Where are you all?" Holly asked.

Smart was programed never to fib, so he said, "Oh hi, Mrs. P. This is Smart. Shannon, Lakoiya and I are speeding through red lights on our way to the recycle center."

"WHAT?" Holly and Shirley shouted.

"Oops, I think I spilled the beans," Smart said.

"Smart," said Shannon. "Text Mom with directions and tell her and Shirley to get over to the recycle center – NOW!!!"

Betty could hear a motor approaching, and then suddenly the metal bin of her prison cell was lifted up and began to move. It was a short ride that ended quickly with a hard landing.

"Okay, the crusher's ready," a worker called out. It was the T Rex all over again. Betty could hear the awful sound of metal being shredded into little pieces, and felt the pots and pans being lifted off her as they were thrown onto the moving belt towards the crusher.

She knew she was next.

At that very moment, the police car was racing up to the recycle center, bracing for a quick stop.

Shannon and Lakoiya jumped out almost before the car came to a halt. As they sprinted towards the recycle center, Shannon called out, "Lakoiya, if we get stopped at the front desk, whoever can get free must find Betty. She's always been terrified of this metal crusher she called the T Rex, and I can hear it! Oh my gosh, Betty will be so scared!"

"No worries, Shannon, I got it. Should we wait for the detectives?"

123

"No, I don't think we have time and I also think we can move faster than those two."

"Yeah," Lakoiya said. "Too many donuts!"

Just as the detectives were getting out of their car, Shirley and Holly zoomed up. "Detectives! Where are the girls?" Holly yelled as she rolled down the window.

Mullins turned around. "There," he said, pointing. They're almost at the front door. Glad you're here! We may need all the help we can get!"

The moms rushed after the detectives into the recycle center.

Shannon and Lakoiya were ahead of them. As they entered, a man with a hard hat and badge came out from behind a counter."Just one moment, young ladies," he said with a hand up, as if to stop them.

Since there was a space to his left, Lakoiya, deciding to act as a decoy, stepped toward the man, giving Shannon the chance to dart to the man's left, jump on a chair, catapult herself over the counter, and disappear into the warehouse.

"Hey! Stop before I call the police!" said the man, who held onto Lakoiya.

Shannon looked back and gave Lakoiya a thumb's-up.

"Hurry, Shannon!" shouted Lakoiya.

"You don't have to call the police, sir," said Detective Mullins. Flashing his badge, he introduced himself and Detective Hardy, then Holly and Shirley.

"Detective, there were two kids. I caught one," said the man, "and the other is somewhere in the recycle center."

"Please release the young lady, sir," Mullins said. "These two girls are police cadets and are in training. They are looking for a friend who was kidnapped."

The man let go of Lakoiya, who took off after Shannon.

"Detective, sir, I haven't seen anyone in the recycle center, and why would they be here anyway?"

"Sir, we are looking for a silver bowl and her name is Betty," said Mullins, sounding very official.

The man with the hard hat stared at the detectives in confusion.

"Don't even ask," said Hardy.

It was a big warehouse, and the noise from T Rex echoed so loudly throughout the building that it was hard to tell where the crusher was located. Lakoiya finally caught up to Shannon and they stopped quickly to catch their breath. Within seconds, the detectives and their moms had joined them.

Smart said, "I think I can turn off the T Rex! I looked up the plans for the recycle center that are on file at the building department. Turn left here!"

"Hurry!" yelled Shannon, and everyone followed Smart, knowing Betty was only seconds away from being crushed.


Betty tried to fly away, but she was so tired and scared she couldn't move. All she could do was call out for Shannon. Not far down the moving belt she could see the other pots and pans being chewed up by T Rex, so she just closed her eyes.

After running into a few dead ends in the big warehouse, Shannon spotted the moving belt. "There!" she yelled.

"Oh my gosh!" screamed Lakoiya. The terrified girls could see Betty just ahead of them, inches away from T Rex's jaws.

Then the belt suddenly stopped. Shannon ran as fast as she could and scooped up Betty, as Smart announced on high volume that he had turned off the T Rex.

Lakoiya ran to Shannon, and they hugged Betty and each other.

Mullins again commended Smart for his great detective work, as Holly told Smart that he'd saved Betty's life.

When Betty composed herself, she opened her eyes and gave a big sigh. She'd thought for sure she was going to end up as scrap metal. "Thank you for saving my life," she said. Looking up at Lakoiya, she asked, "Who is your friend, Shannon?"

"This is Lakoiya. She lives here in the hood, and I would never have found you without her help, and Smart's too."

"Oh, Shannon, I never lost hope that I would see you again," Betty said. "And Lakoiya, thank you for helping to find me."

"No worries," Lakoiya said. "Hey, you are a big silver bowl and you can talk too. I also hear you are a wicked cook. We had to save you!"

Before long the detectives, who now included "Detective Smart," and Holly and Shirley joined Shannon, Betty and Lakoiya.

Holly said, "Shannon, can I give Betty a hug?" Betty flew into Mom's arms.

Mullins looked at Hardy and said, "This was the best lost-and-found case ever!"

As they started to leave, Betty looked back, hoping she'd never see T Rex again. The man in the hard hat waved goodbye, tipped his hat and smiled as they walked out of the center. The Rescue Squad and the detectives shared a round of high fives as they reached the parking lot.

"Let's all go get donuts, I'm buying!" announced Mullins.

The race started again, but this time everyone was laughing as they ran to their cars, wanting to be the first at the donut shop. Smart asked Detective Mullins, "Do you mind if I drive the squad car?" Mullins's face turned bright red. Lost for words, he said, "I'll talk to the chief on that one, Smart."

# Chapter 26

After the much-needed celebration at the donut shop, everyone returned to Shirley and Lakoiya's house and found a place to crash and recharge their batteries, just like Smart.

When Holly realized it was getting late and worried about the traffic heading home -- especially if Smart was going to drive -- she told Shannon they had to say good-bye. Doing so this was much easier for Shannon and Lakoiya, especially since their moms were planning to get together for Thanksgiving dinner.

"Lakoiya, it will be so fun having you over," said Shannon. "I'll show you our garden, our chickens, and I have a bike you can borrow, too."

"Cool," Lakoiya said, "I can't wait,"

Smart jumped into the conversation, informing they'd best get on the road pronto because he hadn't driven at night before. That was all it took for Mom to tell Shirley goodbye and get Shannon and Waddlin in the car.

"Buckle up, everyone," Detective Smart said as he set his GPS for home and turned on an oldies station to soothe Mom's nerves. Soon the little red Bug was on its way, with Waddlin happily sticking her head out the window, Betty on the back seat with the Rescue Squad snuggled up inside her, and Shannon thinking about what a crazy and great day it had been.

"Mom, the hood wasn't all that bad, was it? And we found Betty!"

"You were right, Shannon. It's a cool place and I hope we can go back again soon. I can't believe you and Lakoiya saved Betty's life and we're heading home with her, thanks to our detective friends – including Detective Smart. You know, I've been thinking, I would love to volunteer at that community garden. It's so important for people who struggle with food insecurity to have access to fresh vegetables. I really didn't get it until I saw the urban community garden and learning more about food deserts. Meeting Shirley, Daisy and Lakoiya changed everything for me."

"I'd like to help too, Mom."

"Great, I love that idea," Mom said. "Dad can come along, too. I love Lakoiya and her mom. They feel like a part of our extended family now."

Shannon felt from the beginning Lakoiya was her sister, even though they lived in two different worlds, hood and country. Shannon knew none of that mattered to her or Lakoiya, never, ever!

The hum of the little engine made Shannon sleepy, and before long Detective Smart was the only one awake in the car. He was very proud in that moment, and even though it was just a small VW Bug, he was the captain. Smart took pride in knowing his best friends were in his care.

The sounds of the turn signal and gravel crunching under the tires woke everyone up as they arrived home.

"Thank you, Smart, for getting us here safely," Mom said as the Bug came to a halt at its spot near the trailer. "I still can't believe you drove us home while I was in dreamland, sleeping."

Waddlin jumped out of the car first. When Shannon and Betty finally climbed out, Betty spun out last and so fast that she spilled her cargo into Shannon's arms and took off out of sight over the garden. She was free! It was all coming back to her as she flew around her home. She soared over the small farms that blanketed the area, hoping to see the geese she'd met before. *Oh, what a great feeling! I'm free, I'm home!*

After all they had been through, Shannon was a little worried when she lost sight of Betty, but knew she'd return soon.

The kitchen was alive again with excited chatter, signing, and laughter. It was just like old times. Betty was the only one missing, but Shannon reassured everyone that Betty would be back shortly.

They didn't know at that very moment Betty had the dog door in sight and was aiming at it, like a rocket.

*BOOM!* Betty flew through the dog door, over the couch where Dad was still asleep, and crash-landed on the small kitchen counter.

Shannon grabbed Smart; Left and Right jumped out of the way, and Salt and Pepper flew like bowling pins. Moving quickly, Shannon caught Salt and Pepper in midair just in time.

Betty had arrived!

Everyone was laughing with joy. It was now official. Betty was home again in her kitchen.

After Shannon placed Salt and Pepper and Smart in Betty, Left and Right jumped in and joined the party. Betty grinned, feeling as if a live salad bouncing around inside Betty the bowl.

Hearing the commotion, Shannon's mom hurried into the kitchen. She put her arm around Shannon, kissed her on the forehead, and smiled.

"We're going to make a big feast tonight for dinner," Shannon announced.

Betty excitedly started spinning and the crew talked over each other, discussing the menu. They decided to make spaghetti-squash spaghetti. This was one of Shannon's favorite meals to prepare and eat. She laughed to herself, thinking back to when her mom tried to explain what spaghetti-squash spaghetti was to her. At first Shannon said "no way," but after her mom dug out an old recipe that Grandma Webber wrote years ago on the farm, Shannon learned it was indeed pasta-like strings made from a squash!

As Shannon explained, Smart said, for the first time ever, "I did not know that!" Shannon and her mom looked at him in surprise, and Shannon said, "Well, there's a first time for everything!"

Dinner was made by the crew, enjoyed, and celebrated, Leftovers were packed up in the refrigerator to be relished later so that no food was wasted. Everyone had to digest for a while before dessert was served. Even Waddlin had to take a quick nap before the homemade ice cream (made from Norma's cow's rich cream) and fresh-out-of-the oven cookies hit the table.

As they cooked and cleaned up, Betty heard the full story of the Rescue Squad's secret mission to the big city, and was awestruck that her friends would risk everything to find her. Betty had no idea she was loved so much. Although she felt the love in the past, what her friends had done confirmed what she'd always believed: Betty was now a member of a big, wonderful family.

At the same time, Shannon could see that her mom and dad were having a talk on the couch.

"Honey, I have to tell you something," she heard her mom say nervously.

"Okay, what's up?" her dad asked.

"Well ... honey, I let Smart drive the car." Shannon saw the relief on her mom's face, now she'd said it. She -- and Shannon too -- waited for a comeback, but there was silence.

Then Dad started laughing.

"Why are you laughing?" said Mom in disbelief. "I was so worried to tell you."

"I'm just glad you said it first," Dad said with a big smile.

"What?"

"Well – I have something to tell you. Smart has been driving me around for the past few months."

Mom's mouth dropped open with surprise. She glanced over at Smart, who was on the dining room table. Shannon noticed that his screen had gone dark.

"Smart's a double agent! Oh, you two are in so much trouble," Mom barked. But then she laughed too.

Shannon smiled as her mom and dad kissed and gave each other a big hug. Smart was now in self-exile and checked out for the night.

"You guys are the best," Shannon said, and joined her parents in a three-way hug.

Soon the kitchen crew was stowed away. Shannon's parents were asleep on the couch, and she was bundled up in her sleeping bag, like a burrito, in the backyard hammock. Above her, billions of stars were putting on a light show, including the gift of a lone shooting star. She could have stared at the twinkly sky for hours, but it was a long day and the rocking hammock slowly worked its magic. Soon Shannon fell sound, and happily, asleep. Waddlin was in dreamland too, curled up on her dog bed.

Tonight was just like in the Christmas rhyme: *Not a creature was stirring, not even a mouse.*

# CHAPTER 27

Time passed on the little farm, and before long it was the beginning of fall. The leaves were starting to take on their annual brilliant orange, yellow, and red colors, and shadows were extending their reach into winter. All the summer fruit and veggies had been frozen, canned, or given away to friends and Holly's favorite charities. The garden was bare, but it was storing up its energy for the spring and summer crops.

It was also time for Shannon to head back to school. She thought about how much fun it would be if Lakoiya were in her class someday. Maybe when she was older and ready to go off to college, she would pick a school near the hood and she and Lakoiya could be together.

One day, when Shannon was getting ready to leave for school, her mom said, "We need to plan our Thanksgiving dinner soon, because we've invited Lakoiya, her mom, and Curly, as well as Joe and his family."

"Oh, that's right, Mom, thanks for reminding me! It's going to be a fun Thanksgiving. I can't wait to tell Betty and everyone. They will be so excited to help cook. I know

Betty's always talked about being a part of a big family Thanksgiving."

Betty couldn't believe what she just heard.

"You guys, guess what?" she announced to the Rescue Squad. They could tell by the excitement in Betty's voice this announcement was important. Smart was closing apps as quickly as possible so he could focus on what Betty had to say.

She told the crew about Thanksgiving dinner. "We have to start thinking about ideas for the big party."

She knew who would come up with the most ideas, and expected to hear from Smart any time. The little kitchen was buzzing like a beehive with excitement.

Shannon, meanwhile, headed for the bus stop. She spotted Joe heading down the street just as he spotted her. They both began running and reached the bus at the same time, right before the door closed. All the kids cheered as Shannon and Joe took their seats – watching them run had been like watching an Olympic sprint race on TV.

The bus arrived at school and the kids slowly filed out and made their way to class. Shannon found it difficult to concentrate that day, because she kept thinking about the Thanksgiving feast and giving Lakoiya a tour of the Peterson farm. But the day passed quickly and it was soon time to join everyone on the bus again for the ride home.

"Joe, did you save this spot for me?" Shannon asked as she made her way down the aisle and saw Joe sitting by himself.

Joe managed a shy nod.

Shannon sat down next to him.

Joe looked inside his backpack and produced a small bag. "Shannon, how about some gummy bears?"

"Oh Joe, how did you know I was thinking about how good some gummy bears would be right now?"

"I just knew," he said, blushing.

Shannon smiled and said, "Thank you."

They shared the bag of gummy bears all the way home.

Joe was out the bus door first and had a good lead on Shannon for the race home. She could have caught up easily, but figured Joe needed to win once in a while. She made sure he kept his lead all the way to her driveway.

"Hey, I won!" Joe called as he raised his arms and did a quick victory dance.

Shannon teased that he won because he didn't have much homework and his backpack was lighter than hers.

Joe shook his head. "Victory!" he proclaimed.

*Okay I'll let Joe have the moment of victory I gave him,* thought Shannon. *If I had a little brother, he would be just like Joe.*

She gave Joe a quick shove, laughed, and said, "See you later!" Then they happily went their separate ways.

# CHAPTER 28

When Shannon reached home she was still catching her breath from racing Joe, and was starving. *Maybe when you turn ten you eat more?* she thought, as she flew through the front door and made a beeline for the refrigerator. She hoped something tasty was waiting for her, especially now that Betty was home.

Shannon didn't notice Waddlin lying asleep in her path. She tripped, and almost made it over – which would have been a jump to remember – but the tip of her toe didn't clear Waddlin. *Splat.* Shannon did a face-plant entry into the kitchen.

Mom screeched, then started laughing hysterically. Shannon's face was as red as a ripe tomato as she said, "Hi Mom, I'm home."

Waddlin looked up – *Hmm, no food?* Bummer – and went back to sleep.

After Mom helped Shannon up, they shared a high-five. Shannon found what she was hoping for in the refrigerator – leftover spaghetti-squash spaghetti. She leaned on the kitchen counter like nothing happened and dug in. Sooo ... *good! Sometimes leftovers are the best!*

"Guys," said Mom. "I'm thinking of having a pot-luck-style Thanksgiving dinner. What do you think?"

Shannon and Betty shared an excited look and began talking about what dishes to make.

With a long sigh, Mom added, "Our family food budget is a little short. We have plenty of eggs and vegetables –" she chuckled, "– but we may not be able to afford a turkey this year."

Everyone grinned, for they were all thinking the exact same thing. The rooster out back would be a perfect replacement for the turkey.

Suddenly the rooster crowed: "Cock-a-doodle-dooo!" The timing couldn't have been better.

"He must have overheard our conversation," said Shannon. Everyone laughed, but they couldn't wait to see that big, mean bird on a platter.

As always, Betty was good at keeping things positive and said, "Why don't we think about some fun new recipes for Thanksgiving?"

Shannon grabbed the recipe box containing her grandmother's handwritten recipes and headed into the living room, since when there was more than one person and the Rescue Squad in the tiny trailer kitchen, it was overcrowded. Everyone followed Shannon, who spread recipe cards out on the coffee table. Betty was grinning in delight, but Smart wasn't too happy with the old-fashioned way of looking up recipes, since no one needed his help. Shannon saw his screen go black. *Smart is just like a turtle sticking his head back in his shell,* she thought, and chuckled.

Holding the recipe cards, handwritten by her

grandmother and aunt, was like looking at their old black-and-white photographs. It was a connection to Shannon's past. The handwriting was so beautiful and spoke to Shannon in a very different way from the words on a computer or phone screen. Even though written long ago, the handwritten words felt alive and very real. Shannon could hear her grandmother's and aunt's voices as she read their words.

Shannon felt sad that her good friend Smart would never understand how she felt. Smart was made to live only in the digital world. Shannon knew she wanted to take a writing class in school someday, to honor the past and keep the personal touch of pen to paper alive, just like on her grandmother's and aunt's recipe cards.

A few days before Thanksgiving, Shirley and Mom were trading emails and texting, while Lakoiya and Shannon were on the phone so much that their moms had to limit them to an hour a day. School was now closed for the Thanksgiving holiday, which left the girls with a lot of time to talk.

"I've been thinking, since we don't have our own phones and can't text, why don't we start writing letters, instead of emailing all the time?" Shannon told Lakoiya during one phone call.

"What?" Lakoiya asked.

"Letters," Shannon repeated.

Lakoiya laughed. "I never get letters!"

"That's my point," replied Shannon. "I really like writing in longhand, like my grandparents, aunts and uncles did years ago, before computers and smart phones. Sorry, Smart."

"No worries, Shannon," said Smart. "It's all just digital fonts to me. I also don't have hands to write like you can." He sounded a little sad.

"Lakoiya, don't you think it would be way cool to do something totally different than everyone else at school?" Shannon asked.

Lakoiya thought for a moment. "Yeah, different can be cool."

"Okay, think about this," Shannon said. "Dropping off letters at the post office would be like tossing a message in a bottle into the sea. When the letters arrived in your mailbox, it would be like finding a note in a bottle on a deserted beach."

Lakoiya cracked up.

"I know – trust me on this."

"Okay, sister, I'm in!" Lakoiya said.

"YES!" Shannon shouted. "Lakoiya, you write like your mom paints – beautifully – and you have a cool style. But my handwriting looks like chicken scratch. It's embarrassing. Could you help me with my penmanship?"

"Wow, I never thought of it that way. For sure I'll help you, let's do it!"

"Someday I'd like to be a writer, or a journalist," Shannon said confidently.

"You'd be an amazing writer," Lakoiya said, making sure Shannon knew she believed in her too.

Before long their conversation drifted towards the upcoming feast and farm tour. "Lakoiya, just think of the country as an endless community garden, as far as you can see in any direction. At night the stars are so bright you'd think you can reach up and touch them."

"Wow, I can't wait, Shannon," Lakoiya said. "In the city

you kind of forget about the stars because all the lights block the view of the sky."

Lakoiya believed one of those bright stars was now her dad. She told Shannon, "When I'm at your house in the country and we're looking at all the stars, I want to name one after my dad."

"I love that idea," Shannon said, thinking how lucky she was to have her dad. Then she had an idea. "Hold on, let me ask Smart a question. I think there's an app you can get that identifies stars. You just point your smart phone to the sky and click. It will tell you what stars are above. It would be easy to name one after your dad and you'll be able to find your dad's star anytime."

"Yes there is such an app and it's free!" said Smart.

"No way!" Lakoiya said excitedly.

"Now all you need is a phone like Smart," said Shannon.

"I can borrow my mom's!" Lakoiya said.

"Make sure you ask first," Shannon said, and they rolled their eyes and smiled.

After a moment, Shannon thought she heard a sniffle. "Lakoiya, are you okay?" she asked.

"I really miss my dad sometimes," Lakoiya whispered, "even though I never met him."

Shannon wasn't sure what to say, but really wanted to help Lakoiya. So, she thought a bit and then said, "How about we invite him to our Thanksgiving dinner?"

"How do we do that?" Lakoiya asked.

Shannon knew she could make a big difference in her friend's life. She explained that on special occasions, like birthdays and holidays, she and her mom would bring out all the hand-me-down tablecloths, napkins, old platters and bowls from past generations. The patchwork of history made it feel as if the whole family was together again.

"Bring your favorite photo of your dad and place it where you're sitting, and he'll be right next to you, enjoying Thanksgiving dinner. I'll bring photos of my grandparents, aunts, and uncles to set on the table too. We'll be one big happy family!"

"And when it gets dark, I can show everyone my dad's star!" Lakoiya said.

Instantly, Shannon felt a change in Lakoiya and could hear it in her voice. Her best friend was happy again, which made Shannon happy and thankful too.

# CHAPTER 29

On the day before Thanksgiving, everyone was busy with chores in the little silver trailer and garden. Smart was supplying music for Shannon and her mom, this time reggae, in honor of Lakoiya and her mom's favorite music. Shannon and her mom couldn't help dancing and singing to the fun rhythms as they cleaned the trailer.

"Mom, where did you learn to dance like that?" Shannon joked.

"Oh, your dad swept me off my feet on the dance floor one night years ago, and we became dance partners for life."

"No way – you and Dad used to dance." Shannon smirked.

"Yep," Mom said with a big smile while spinning on her toes.

By the time lunch came around, they were tired and hungry. Mom suggested deviled-egg sandwiches because she'd seen a lot of fresh eggs in the laying boxes earlier in the day.

As always, Smart was happy to supply several recipes

for deviled-egg sandwiches. Everyone said at the same time, "Thank you, Smart."

Mom asked Shannon to fetch the eggs.

"Okay, Mom," she said, sprinting off to the chicken coop.

The Rescue Squad was delighted they hadn't been asked to collect the eggs. One time was enough in the big rooster's house.

The eggs in the laying boxes were large and beautiful: green, gold, tan, brown, and white. Shannon knew which hens were laying, because each hen had a favorite laying box. In the blink of an eye, Shannon's wire basket was filled with fresh eggs. She held it in front of her to make sure the big rooster knew not to mess with her as she left the chicken coop.

When Shannon returned, everyone was ready to help prepare lunch. The large loaf of cheese bread Mom had made the day before was waiting to be sliced, and a pot of water was already boiling. Left and Right quickly washed the eggs to remove the "chocolate" (as chicken poop was called in the country). Shannon gently added the eggs to the boiling water. Betty and Left and Right were ready to peel the eggs when they had finished cooking.

Smart was a little upset because they didn't need any of his recipes. Shannon said deviled-egg sandwiches were simple – eggs, mayo, salt and pepper. Salt and Pepper overheard Shannon and said out loud, "Did we hear our names? We are happy to shake anytime!"

Shannon was going to have a little fun with everyone, but first she had to ask Smart a favor.

"Okay, I know you know the answer, so promise you won't say anything, Smart, please?"

He reluctantly agreed, knowing what Shannon was going to say.

"Okay, guys, before Left and Right peel the eggs, how do you tell a fresh egg from a hardboiled egg?" Shannon asked.

Left and Right signed, "Break one?"

Everyone laughed.

Betty said, "Put one under a light?"

"No, but nice try."

Salt and Pepper said, "Who cares?"

Shannon sighed and gave them the look.

The kitchen went silent and Shannon knew she had them. She picked up two eggs. She spun the first one, and it whirled like a top. She spun the second egg, and it wobbled around on the counter like a chicken with a sore foot.

No one said anything, but Smart started vibrating with excitement, because he knew the answer. Shannon turned and gave him the look, too. "The cookie jar is in reach," she reminded Smart.

"You wouldn't," said Smart.

"Oh yes I would," Shannon shot back, and started to reach for the cookie jar lid.

Smart turned himself off. This was his way of saying, "I'm done with this conversation."

*Smart can be such a brat sometimes. Maybe that's why he's so much fun to have around!*

All of a sudden Betty said, "I know! The egg that spins is the hardboiled egg. The uncooked one wobbles because the yoke and white are floppy liquid!"

Everyone cheered when Shannon said, "That's right! Okay, I'm getting hungry. Let's peel the eggs."

Left and Right were faster than anyone in the kitchen at peeling, and not a single bit of eggshell was left on the hard-boiled eggs. Shannon added a little mayo, then Salt and Pepper did their shake over the eggs, and then the mixture was plopped onto Mom's beautiful, homemade, toasted cheese bread.

Looking out the kitchen window, Shannon noticed how beautiful the orchard was today. "Hey, let's all eat out in the orchard before the fall colors say goodbye for another season."

The crew made their way through the orchard leaves, which were now over their ankles. The leaves danced in the wind and instantly covered up every step along the way. Shannon said, "It's like walking on the beach when a wave covers up your footprints forever."

As Shannon finished lunch, they discussed that since there would be extra guests this year for Thanksgiving, and the trailer was so small, they should find another place on the farm to have the big dinner. Smart told everyone the weather forecast predicated a seasonally warm Thanksgiving Day with no rain in sight.

Shannon thought for a moment. "Let's take a vote on where we want to have our Thanksgiving dinner."

Smart tallied the votes and it was unanimous. The orchard! Shannon was delighted with the results. *Yeah! I love this orchard, and our homegrown apples that will be going into Mom's apple pies. It's going to be the best Thanksgiving ever!*

At their home, Shirley and Lakoiya spent the morning together before Thanksgiving at the community garden. It seemed like everyone in the neighborhood had been there throughout the day. The old trees were giving everyone a last gift of brilliant fall colors, just like on the Peterson's little country farm. Another chapter in trees' lives was ending, and a well-deserved rest was just ahead. All the urban farmers loved the big trees that shaded some of the garden during the sweltering heat of summer, bringing a little bit of the country to the neighborhood.

Today, unlike most days, the community garden was like a mini farmers' market, with everyone picking what they needed to make their Thanksgiving dinners special. No money was exchanged, just hugs, smiles and stories, and recipes that had been handed down from one generation to the next. In many ways, it was exactly what Thanksgiving was all about, giving thanks for the bounty of homegrown food. The good vibes were evident today, with a bumper crop of community unity and love.

Shirley and Lakoiya left the garden with a basket full of fresh vegetables and their hearts overflowing with Thanksgiving cheer. As they said their goodbyes, Lakoiya said to her mom, "This was so much better than going to the supermarket!"

Back in their kitchen, mother and daughter turned up the radio and sang along with some great gospel soul music, which they thought was very fitting just before Thanksgiving. They were excited and proud to share some of their family favorite holiday food with their new friends.

Shirley said to Lakoiya, "I can't wait to lift the lids off the dishes and tell everyone about Grandma's fixings, including this sweet potato pie and collard greens."

# CHAPTER 30

There's something very special about Thanksgiving morning. Upon waking it feels a bit like Christmas. Both days have gifts waiting to be enjoyed, but on Thanksgiving morning you can smell the gifts cooking in the kitchen and working their way through your home. The excitement comes from the anticipation of spending all day with your family and favorite friends, and eating with them.

Betty and the Rescue Squad had been up almost all night, cooking. In the morning, they continued the cooking Olympics.

"You guys deserve a gold medal. We're almost ready – don't stop now," Betty told her friends, just like a coach.

Left and Right could barely keep up with cleaning the pots and pans, Smart was making sure recipes were followed, Betty was spinning and mixing, and Salt and Pepper yipped in Spanish and helped with the seasoning. It was organized chaos, but fun. Betty reminisced back to when she and her buddies were on the thrift store sale rack, worried they wouldn't be able to stay together, let alone find a forever home. Now here they all were, in a tiny country kitchen, cooking an amazing Thanksgiving dinner.

With all the noise, Waddlin figured it would be a good idea to plop down right in the middle of the floor in case she was needed for a cleanup.

Shannon appeared in the kitchen next. She stepped over Wadd, and couldn't believe her eyes. "You guys are amazing!" she shouted out over the chaos. She knew today was going to be a special day, and it would be even better when everyone was sitting at the picnic tables in the orchard.

When Shannon's mom stumbled into the kitchen, with morning bed-head hair and looking in desperate need of coffee, she found a cup waiting for her on the counter -- an early Thanksgiving gift from Shannon.


This Thanksgiving would be very different for Shirley and Lakoiya. For the first time, they wouldn't be home. Shirley was worried that someone who didn't have a place to go for Thanksgiving might stop by, so she left a note on the front door. It told anyone who was hungry to go a few doors down to Myrna's house for a big plate of Thanksgiving food and love.

An Uber car pulled into the driveway. As Shirley greeted him, Lakoiya smiled and thought about what fun it would've been if the Uber's driver had been Smart. To her surprise, Curly was in the car's front seat, looking handsome in a bow tie and hat. He had even shaved, and smelled like the barbershop downtown.

"Curly, you're looking so handsome," said Shirley. "We need to get you a date next year. You know, I was talking to Daisy the other day and she had so many nice things to say about you. If you're a friend of Daisy, you're a friend of ours."

Curly tipped his hat, smiled at Lakoiya and Shirley and said, "Thank you, and I'm very lucky to have two beautiful dates today."

Lakoiya laughed. "I'm definitely going to set you up with Daisy next Thanksgiving."

"Well, that would be very nice indeed, young lady," Curly said. "Daisy's an angel."

Across the street from Shannon's, Joe was helping his parents make sourdough bread. His mom had a starter yeast recipe that had been passed down for generations and was considered a family heirloom. But Joe's mind was really on something else. Like everyone who was invited to Shannon's house, he was excited. But Joe was nervous, too. He wanted to sit by Shannon at dinner, but didn't know how.

*I can't just ask her*, he kept thinking. Just the thought of it made him a little squeamish. Then it hit him. He would write a note and have the drone deliver it! "Brilliant!" he said out loud.

"Brilliant, Joe?" his mom asked from another room. "Did you get a good grade at school?"

*Rats*, Joe thought, *Mom she can hear everything*. He had no time to spare, and Mom was taking up valuable time.

"Yes, Mom," he said, hoping that would be the end of the questions.

"Oh, good, honey – I'm so proud of you."

Joe grinned and replied, "Thanks, Mom," then went back to writing Shannon's note. After three attempts (after all, it was the most important note of his life) he got it just right. Then he attached it to his drone and turned on its two-way speaker-camera so he'd be able to talk to Shannon.

Joe, who'd been masterminding this drone invitation mission since he'd found out his family was invited to the Petersons' for Thanksgiving, hurried up to his bedroom -- his mission control tower. WIth the President and Vice President (his dad and mom) none the wiser, Joe launched the drone from the driveway below and directed it toward the Petersons' trailer.

Joe had planned to circle the drone out of sight above the trailer, but today was a bit windy. He'd have to be extra careful not to crash and have his plan bite the dust. As the drone approached the trailer, Joe carefully lowered it to window level, right outside the kitchen, cleared his throat, and made an announcement on the speaker: "Shannon, this is Joe speaking."

No response.

*Hmmm*, Joe thought, *I wonder where Shannon is?*

He turned up the volume. "Shannon, are you in the kitchen?"

Still nothing. In his mission control tower, Joe began to worry.

Smart heard Joe first. Smart was on the spice shelf and was looking out the window as the drone flew by.

*Who was speaking?* Smart wondered. Then he figured out Joe's plan and started to laugh.

Salt and Pepper started yipping, "Eye yi yi!" because they were sure they'd just seen an alien spaceship. Smart assured them it was just Joe's drone – the one he'd flown on their rescue mission – but they didn't believe him, and started shaking all over. Then they hid in the cupboard.

Just before Shannon walked into the kitchen, a gust

of wind roared over the trailer, sweeping the drone away like a fallen leaf. It flew right into a tree. Everyone heard the crash but had no idea what it was – except Smart.

"Rats!" Joe said. The camera screen had gone blank. He'd just lost his new drone. But he was actually more worried that he'd now have to ask Shannon the BIG question in person.

Joe dropped the drone controls, ran out of his room and right into his mom. He bounced off her, and would have fallen head first down the stairs had she not grabbed his arm at the last second.

"What are you doing, Joe?" she asked.

Joe kept on moving and answered, "My drone just crashed at Shannon's house!"

"Oh Joe, it's brand new!"

Joe made it to Shannon's faster than ever before. He was just rounding the back of the little silver trailer where he thought his drone had crashed, when he ran smack into Shannon. In one hand she had the smashed drone, and in the other, the note. Joe's stomach flipped and his heart raced. What could he say?

"Joe, wow. I like your note. How did you know I love handwritten notes and letters? Lakoiya and I write to each other by hand all the time. Yes, it would be cool to sit next to you at dinner. My friend Lakoiya will be sitting with us too."

All Joe could do was stare at his feet.

"Joe? Are you okay?"

When he finally collected himself, he muttered, "Thanks," collected his messed up drone, and took off. But as he ran back home, his stride was light and his spirit bright.

"Don't be late, Joe!" Shannon called out after him.

# CHAPTER 31

A short time later, Shannon heard a car bumping up the dirt driveway. It was Lakoiya, her mom, and Curly, and she couldn't wait to show them the farm. She jumped over Waddlin, who also heard the car approaching. Smart smiled and filmed as Waddlin jumped to her feet, toenails scrabbling on the slick kitchen floor, like an ice skater – but not quite as graceful.

Before the dust had settled, Lakoiya was out of the car, running to meet Shannon. It seemed like such a long time since they'd seen each other. There were big hugs and lots of laughs.

Shirley got out, stretched, and then gathered up the special Thanksgiving dishes. Curly stood looking around, as if he'd been here before. He closed his eyes and took a deep breath of sweet country air.

In the trailer kitchen, Left was holding up Salt so he could look out the window and report to the crew what was happening outside. Introductions and more hugs took place as Shannon's mom and dad joined in. Everyone helped carry the amazing food into the trailer.

There were cries of, "Oh, look at that!" and "Wow, that smells so good!" A few hands were playfully slapped away as they tried to steal an early bite.

The little kitchen suddenly felt closet-sized as everyone organized the food. Counter space was at a premium, and the kitchen began to sound like the chicken coop when excited hens started cackling. Everyone quickly learned the small kitchen pivot dance, along with the art of stepping over Waddlin.

The Rescue Squad was reunited with Lakoiya and Curly, and then again introduced to Shirley. She didn't look at all surprised to see salad tossing hands walking on the counter, and salt and pepper shakers chattering in Spanish. After all, somewhere in this group was a mobile phone that could drive a car!

Betty thought, *What a miracle – my family and friends are finally all together.* She gave thanks again that she wasn't forgotten, and hadn't been turned into scrap metal by T Rex.

Smart was supplying the music and taking pictures and video of everyone organizing the platters and bowls of food. He began to think he might like to direct films in Hollywood someday. Left and Right were busy mixing and tossing.

Holly picked up Salt and Pepper and turned to Shannon and Lakoiya. "Would you girls place Salt and Pepper on the picnic table outside? And then, Shannon, why don't you give Lakoiya a little farm tour?"

"Okay, Mom," Shannon said. "Come on, Lakoiya."

Together the girls went outside and placed Salt and Pepper in the middle of the long picnic table, right next to a big bouquet of fresh cut flowers buzzing with the occasional friendly bee. "Remember when we were tossed in the trash can?" said Salt to Pepper. "Look at us now, in the center of this beautiful Thanksgiving table."

Lakoiya looked around, eyes wide. The turquoise, red, and yellow picnic tables seemed to be sitting in the middle of an outdoor cathedral, thanks to the big old trees that silently smiled and were proud to host their first Thanksgiving meal.

"So this is what the country looks like," Lakoiya said.

Shannon could tell Lakoiya, who was still as a morning pond, was taking it all in, which made Shannon happy. Except for the little songs of the country -- the wind whistling through the orchard, and Norma's cows mooing in harmony somewhere in the distance -- the beautiful day was wrapped up like a present in gentle silence.

"Shannon, this is sooo fine," Lakoya said, gazing into the distance.

Shannon then took Lakoiya to the hen house to introduce her to all the beautiful hens, including her favorites: Roberta the Road Island Red, Alice the Araconda, and Winny the Black Laced Wyondot.

Lakoiya said jokingly, "So this is where eggs come from." Shannon nodded as Lakoiya added, "This is way better than buying eggs from a store."

Lakoiya found the big, fluffy hens beautiful, and had the best time gathering the multi-colored eggs. She told Shannon they amazed her, because she'd never seen colored eggs before – only white ones. Shannon decided that later, her city friends would leave with a dozen eggs each, as well as an extra dozen for Daisy, her friend from the community garden.

Shannon and Lakoiya continued the tour down a

well-worn path towards the family garden. Waddlin, nose to the ground, was just a step ahead of them. As they walked, Shannon knew it was time for the hens to be let loose in the garden to pick and scratch now that the garden was taking a rest from a busy spring and summer. The chickens would leave behind some beneficial fertilizer, better known as chicken poop. Shannon looked back over her shoulder and saw all the hens lined up, looking towards the garden.

She said out loud, "Don't worry, I'll let you out to play soon."

Lakoiya asked, "Who are you talking to, Shannon?"

"Oh, just the hens."

Shannon told Lakoiya that it was the time of year when the garden was put to bed for the winter. With a little love and lots of effort, it would be a sea of green come spring. Some of the beds were already turned over and ready for the annual planting. The rest were in the stage of natural soil composting. The bugs and microorganisms were busy at work tending their home in the garden.

Lakoiya remarked that it wasn't much different from how the community garden looked yesterday. Then they heard a familiar humming sound, and Betty dropped out of the sky and did a perfect landing between the two girls. Lakoiya started laughing out loud. Left and Right jumped out of Betty and started to run around the garden. They needed a little fresh air after all the work in the kitchen.

"Hey, Shannon."

She turned around to find Joe in a white, buttoned-down shirt, crooked little bow tie, and sporting his new Vans sneakers. He bravely gave Shannon a big hug.

"Hey, Joe," Shannon said. "This is Lakoiya, my new friend from the city."

"Hey, Lakoiya. Happy Thanksgiving," Joe said.

"Happy Thanksgiving, Joe." Lakoiya smiled back. "Was your drone the one we used to help find Betty?"

"Yep," Joe said with a big smile. He had his new repaired drone with him, and showed it to Shannon and Lakoiya. "Do you want to fly it around the farm?" he asked.

Shannon knew this was a big deal for Joe. "We would love to. Let me get Smart so he can go for a ride."

"Wow, great idea," Joe said.

Shannon and Lakoiya sent Smart on a roller coaster ride five hundred feet above the little farm.

Joe was amazed. "You guys are pretty good at that!"

Shannon said, "Yep," and handed the controls back to Joe with a big grin and a wink, because she knew it was really Smart who was piloting the drone.

After a while Betty announced it was almost time to serve up the Thanksgiving feast.

Shannon and Lakoiya looked at each other and said, "I'm starving!"

Shannon took off, running toward the trailer, with Lakoiya and Joe right behind her, Betty and Smart zooming behind them, and Waddlin bringing up the rear.

# CHAPTER 32

Everyone was happy to help bring the homemade food to the picnic tables set up in the orchard cathedral. Lakoiya, holding her favorite photograph of her father to set beside her, gently helped Curly to the table. Shannon did the same thing with favorite pictures of her grandparents and other family members.

Curly said, "I'm so proud of you honoring your father, Lakoiya. He says thank you, and sends his love."

Lakoiya squeezed Curly's hand, trusting every word he said.

Shannon said, "Joe, come sit between Lakoiya and me."

Joe couldn't believe he was going to sit between two cute girls. He thought *Okay, don't do anything stupid like trip*. When he got to his seat (without tripping), David whispered, "Joe – no aftershave. Good call."

Joe confidently gave David a thumb's-up, acknowledging their man-to-man talk at the BBQ.

Betty was in the middle of the Thanksgiving table, filled with a fresh organic garden salad that Left and Right were tossing. Salt and Pepper were dancing around to the festive music Smart was again supplying.

Shannon saw her dad walking towards the picnic table carrying a covered tray. He placed it next to her and took off the cover. To everyone's surprise, the Thanksgiving bird was on the small side.

Holly said suspiciously, "That does not look like a turkey."

David didn't say a word. He just looked at Shannon and winked. Right then, Shannon knew who the bird of honor was. She looked down at Waddlin and patted her on the head. In a quiet voice she said, "Waddlin, a little extra bird for you today."

Curly stood up. "I would like to give thanks to God for such a perfect day and for such a lovely gift of friends and food. I'm also honored we have many relatives joining us, along with a special family member, Don, Lakoiya's dad. He is our hero, and I know for sure he loves you all very much and is here with us today." Curly looked at Lakoiya, who had the biggest smile on her face. Then he looked at Shannon and winked. "I'd also like to recognize that through Betty, we all found each other, and I have faith that this is a start of an orchard Thanksgiving tradition for years to come."

Betty wanted to fly over the orchard in celebration, but she was full of today's monster salad! Then she thought, *I am so thankful, and this is exactly where I want to be, surrounded by family and friends and an amazing home-cooked Thanksgiving meal.*

Without a word being said, everyone held hands and bowed their heads. Waddlin placed her chin on Shannon's leg. Left and Right signed as Curly prayed the most amazing grace.

# CHAPTER 33

It was a few days after the Thanksgiving feast, and Shannon and her mom were washing up after a late lunch of amazing leftovers. Betty was drying on the kitchen counter, and Left and Right were enjoying a swim in the dishwater. Salt and Pepper had started their daily siesta in the spice rack. Smart was being charged and was feeling more energetic by the minute.

Shannon and her mom were surprised to see a car turning into their driveway.

"Who could this be?" Holly said.

Shannon was on her tiptoes trying to see out the kitchen window, but could barely see the car. Waddlin was already heading out the trailer to greet their guests. Betty flew along, right behind her.

As Waddlin reached the car, and Betty made a perfect landing on its roof, Shirley, Lakoiya and Curly emerged. Lakoiya greeted Waddlin with a big kiss on her head while Shirley retrieved something from the back of the car.

Curly said, "Hello, Betty!" as he reached over and picked her up. "Nice to see you again, beautiful." Betty was so happy to be in Curly's loving arms.

"Mom, they must like our farm," Shannon said as she rushed out of the trailer to greet her friends. It was a true hug fest. The extended family was back together again.

As they stood around talking, Shirley's phone rang and she quickly checked who was calling. She turned bright red, answered, and said, "Hi, Hardy – let me call you right back."

Holly looked at Shirley in shock, which turned into a big grin.

Shirley reached into the car and brought out a large, flat package, which she handed to Holly. "We were so devastated when we lost Lakoiya's dad, but we have a new extended family to share our lives with. We love you all so much! I call this painting *The First Supper*."

Shirley had envisioned the painting in her mind as soon as she walked into the country cathedral on Thanksgiving. I have to paint this moment, she had told herself that day. She'd captured the multi-colored hand-me-down tablecloths, the photographs of family, fresh-cut flowers, beautiful food, and smiles all around. She'd also included a star in the sky above.

"Mom, how did you know about the star?" Lakoiya asked.

Shirley just looked at Curly.

Suddenly, everyone heard the buzzing sound of a drone.

Shannon started laughing and shouted, "Hey, Joe, glad you could make it!"

A voice from the drone said, "Shannon, how did you know it was me?"

"Lucky guess!" Shannon yelled back.

Joe responded, "Sorry I'm not over at your house. I'm studying for a big test in my science class. I really hope to be an engineer someday, and design drones that can fly on the moon in zero gravity. I saw you all together from my bedroom window and wanted to hang out, too! Hey, Shannon, do you want to go to the moon with me someday?"

Shannon rolled her eyes, grinned and said, "Sure, Joe – but only if I can bring Waddlin!"

The friends all welcomed Joe hovering above. Everybody came together in a big group hug, all saying and signing with joy, "This Thanksgiving was a true masterpiece!"

# Epilogue

Twenty years later, two moms, Shannon and Lakoiya, were sitting in Shannon's house, reading the letters they wrote as kids out loud and laughing hysterically, when their daughters, Sage and Kellie, joined them.

Lakoiya's daughter, Sage, asked, "What are you reading?"

Shannon's daughter, Kellie, added, "And what's so funny?"

Lakoiya gave the girls the look her own mom used to give her. "Shannon and I are reading letters we wrote to each other when we were about your age."

"Letters?" asked Sage.

"We never get letters. Post office? What's that about?" laughed Kellie.

Shannon and Lakoiya looked at each other. They didn't have to say a word –they knew exactly what the other was thinking.

"Hey, you two," Shannon said, "let's go in the kitchen and bake a big batch of shortbread cookies ... or maybe Meyer lemon bars!" The moms knew the time was right to introduce the Rescue Squad to their daughters and have a little fun at the same time.

"Sage," Lakoiya said, "please open the cupboard above you. There's a big silver bowl we'll use for mixing."

"Okay, Mom," Sage happily replied.

Lakoiya and Shannon took a step back, anticipating what would happen next. Sage pulled up a small stool and stood on it to reach the cupboard. When she opened it, Betty flew out and circled above everyone in the kitchen. Sage yelped and jumped off the stool into her mom's arms while Kellie's mouth dropped open. Betty made a perfect landing on the kitchen counter.

"Girls, this is our friend Betty," Shannon said.

Sage, catching her breath, said, "I thought it was a flying saucer!"

Lakoiya and Shannon just beamed, since they'd heard that very thing a long time ago.

"Hi, Sage. Hi, Kellie," Betty said.

"Mom, how does the bowl know our names?" Kellie asked, looking a little confused.

"Kellie, her name is Betty and I have known her longer than I've known you," Shannon said in a kind and reassuring voice.

"Me, too!" said Lakoiya.

Then, out of the blue, another voice spoke out. "I found some recipes for shortbread cookies, also known as shortbread biscuits."

"Who said that?!" Kellie and Sage asked at the same time, looking even more confused. Smart was leaning up next to the cookie jar on the counter.

"This is another of our good friends; his name is Smart," said Shannon.

"Mom," said Kellie, "that is the oldest, most outdated smart phone I have ever seen!"

Shannon cringed, knowing this probably wouldn't go over very well with Smart. Indeed, she saw his screen shutting down. Oh no, he turned into a turtle again.

"And we have four more friends to introduce you to as well," Lakoiya announced.

"Four more?" Sage and Kellie asked.

"Yep!" Shannon and Lakoiya said together.

Jumping off the dish-drying rack and walking towards them were Left and Right, moving around like they were dancing, and Salt and Pepper, chattering in Spanish. Shannon and Lakoiya informed the girls that the hands were actually "signing," and their daughters said they wanted to learn that language as well.

"Don't forget to preheat the oven," Smart suddenly announced.

Sage and Kellie looked even more surprised that the phone was talking without being given a command, but by this point they looked as if they believed that anything could happen.

Before long, everyone was enjoying shortbread cookies and lemon bars. And the moms shared with their daughters how two girls from different worlds, one from the country and one from the hood, met and became lifelong best friends ... all because of a loving silver bowl named Betty.

# AUTHOR'S NOTE

In loving memory of my sister Shannon Bernice Delaney and my brother Joseph Delaney, both of whom I never met but was able to spend a little time with while writing this story. They now have a voice. Another thanks to my grandmother, Bernice Webber, for letting me spend many summers in her vegetable and flower garden as a child. This was the start of my love of food.

I need to give a very special thanks to my best friend and wife, Holly, for her patience and help while I wrote this story.

Mom, you were in my thoughts every day as well. This is as much your story as mine.

A big thanks to Susan Schader for her amazing editing.

Another big thanks to Nadia Ronquillo, illustrator extraordinaire.

Thank you to all my good friends and family who've encouraged me and my wandering mind, kept my spirits high, along with keeping my hands on the key board.

Kellie Delaney, Patty Dedrick, Happy LaShelle, Aidan Terry, Ryan McCabe, Kacey Meairs, Lida Sideris, Heidi Honeyman. Please forgive me if I left someone out. Another senior moment!

166